"Where Do You Get All Your Animals?" Lyn Asked.

"From the pound, mostly," Casey said. "You'd be surprised what people throw out with the garbage."

"So," Lyn said softly, "you do care."

He was surprised. "What?"

"You said your animals were just a job and you never got attached to them. But I think you're just an old softie at heart."

That made him uncomfortable. Casey was not used to people analyzing him. But because it was Lyn, because the quiet, open way she looked at him suggested a kind of intimacy he had never expected from her, he was taken off guard. He didn't feel threatened, he felt . . . touched. Pleased. And he couldn't push her away, not entirely.

The smile that curved his lips was wistful. "Honey, I haven't been attached to anyone or anything since I was a kid. I don't think I'm capable of it anymore." He looked at her, and his eyes held a quiet honesty with no regret. "You should remember that."

Dear Reader:

Sensuous, emotional, compelling...these are all words that describe Silhouette Desire. If this is your first Desire novel, let me extend an invitation for you to revel in the pleasure of a tantalizing, fulfilling love story. If you're a regular reader, you already know that you're in for a treat!

A Silhouette Desire can encompass many varying moods and tones. The story can be deeply moving and dramatic, or charming and lighthearted. But no matter what, each and every Silhouette Desire is a terrific romance written by and for today's woman.

April is a special month here at Silhouette Desire. First, there's *Warrior,* one of Elizabeth Lowell's books in the *Western Lovers* series. And don't miss *The Drifter* by Joyce Thies, April's *Man of the Month,* which is sure to delight you.

Paula Detmer Riggs makes her Silhouette Desire debut with *Rough Passage,* an exciting story of trust and love. Rounding out April are wonderful stories by Laura Leone, Donna Carlisle and Jessica Barkley. There's something for everyone, every mood, every taste.

So give in to Desire...you'll be glad you did.

All the best,

Lucia Macro
Senior Editor

DONNA CARLISLE
FOR KEEPS

SILHOUETTE *Desire*®

Published by Silhouette Books New York

America's Publisher of Contemporary Romance

SILHOUETTE BOOKS
300 East 42nd St., New York, N.Y. 10017

FOR KEEPS

ISBN: 0-373-05634-6

First Silhouette Books printing April 1991

DONNA CARLISLE

lives in Atlanta, Georgia, with her teenage daughter. Weekends and summers are spent in her rustic north Georgia cabin, where she enjoys hiking, painting and planning her next novel. Donna has also written under the pseudonyms Rebecca Flanders and Leigh Bristol.

To Shannon and Libby,
of course

One

"Come on, Pat, will you lighten up?" Lyn Sanders kept her tone playful but her exasperation was not entirely feigned. "How hard can it be?"

A worried frown played around her sister's brow as she wedged her overnight bag between the two larger cases in the Honda's small trunk. Pat was only going to be gone for a week but, in the true Boy Scout spirit, had packed enough to be prepared for anything.

"It's not that I don't think you can handle the job," Pat assured her, straightening up as she closed the trunk. "It's just that you've only been here a couple of weeks and I feel rotten running out on you like this..."

Lyn laughed and hugged her sister with one arm. "That's the whole point, isn't it? You haven't had a vacation in six years, now I'm here to take care of the business so will you go, already, and have a good time? It's a quarter till eight and you were supposed to pick up Marilee at seven-thirty."

"Oh, no." This new concern added another worry line to Pat's forehead as she hurried to the driver's door. "She's so compulsive she'll have the state patrol out looking for me in another five minutes. I don't know how I'm going to stand driving all the way to North Carolina with her."

"*She's* compulsive?" Lyn gave an exaggerated lift of her eyebrows. "Sounds to me like the pot calling the kettle black."

Pat opened the door and paused, smiling. But this time the concern in her eyes had nothing to do with the business she was leaving in her younger sister's hands. "Are you sure you're going to be all right? Because if you need me to stay—"

"I'm going to be fine," Lyn assured her firmly. And as she saw the doubt in Pat's eyes she added more gently, "This is just what I need, really. To be alone for a while, and sort things out. I'll have plenty to keep me busy, and that's the best therapy in the world. So please, just have a good time and *don't worry*."

"If you say so."

The two sisters embraced, and Lyn stepped away from the car as Pat got in and started the engine. "Drive carefully," she called. "Be sure to call me from the hotel."

Pat waved, put the car in gear, and then stopped abruptly, leaning her head out the window. "Did I tell you about Casey Carmichael?"

"You told me, you told me!" Lyn started backing toward the house.

"And you won't forget where the city maps are and the emergency numbers and—"

"Will you for heaven's sake *go*?"

Pat hesitated, then gave her sister an apologetic smile as she shifted to drive and released the brake. "I'll call you tonight," she promised.

"Have a good time," Lyn repeated.

Pat waved as she drove off, but Lyn did not release her breath of relief until the little blue car was out of the driveway and had disappeared down the street.

Sometimes Lyn wondered whether she, or Pat, or both might be adopted, for never had two sisters been less alike. Pat was eight years older than Lyn, but the difference was more than that. Pat was orderly, reliable, conservative; she always had control of her life and everything in her environment. Lyn waded through life an hour late and a dollar short, and had never, as far back as she remembered, been in control of anything. Composure was something she had always wished she had, and poise was a word people used to describe Pat, not her younger sister.

The two women did not even look alike. Pat was small and neat, blond, and managed to look perfectly groomed even in a sweatshirt and gardening gloves. Lyn was tall and slim with a mass of shoulder length, curly red hair that tended to frizz in the Florida humidity. Her features were as delicate as her sister's, and her complexion even fairer, but she had never troubled to learn the art of making the most of what she had with the use of makeup. Her broad high forehead and widely set gray eyes gave her a strikingly Nordic look, while her delicately shaped mouth and nose suggested a fragility that was completely out of place with the rest of her appearance. Lyn's mother used to say that Lyn's was a haunting face, a memorable one; Lyn had translated that to mean plain. Pat was the pretty one. And though it was true that men rarely forgot Lyn's face, it was Pat they fell in love with.

That used to bother Lyn, even though the two sisters were too far apart in age to compete for the same boyfriends. Now that Lyn had reached the relative wisdom of twenty-eight years, she was only glad that she did not have to worry about keeping herself beautiful for a string of suitors on top of everything else.

She went back into the house and quickly rinsed the coffee cups and left them to drain, then went into the small home office that served as Pet Pride's headquarters. Pat had started the pet-sitting business seven years ago, after her husband's death, and though it was far from becoming a Fortune 500 company—most months, in fact, it barely made a profit—Pat was justifiably proud of it. She had a long-standing list of faithful clients who relied upon her to take care of their pets and their homes while they were away, many of whom were prominent citizens.

In January, however, few people left Florida to take vacations, and the pet-sitting business was slow. Pet Pride had two jobs scheduled for the week, each of which Lyn was familiar with down to the last detail, having accompanied Pat for three days in a row while she made her rounds. There were the Greshams' cats—three snobbish Persians who ate hand-prepared meals that had to be warmed to a precise temperature in the microwave and whose immaculate coats required brushing and de-matting twice a day—and Mr. Jolly's three saltwater aquariums and one basset hound.

Then, of course, there was this Casey Carmichael, who had had the temerity to call at six-thirty in the morning to schedule a job beginning that day. Apparently he was a regular, because Pat had not hesitated about accepting, and she had chattered on and on about the particulars of the job while rushing back and forth with last-

minute preparations for her trip. Lyn, more concerned
with getting her sister out of the house before she changed
her mind than with irrelevant details, had paid little attention. Pat was as compulsive about record keeping as
she was about everything else, and whatever Lyn needed
to know would be found in Casey Carmichael's file.

The Carmichael file—actually a tabbed and indexed
spiral notebook similar to the one Pat kept for all her
regulars—was on top of the desk, squarely centered beneath the lamps so that Lyn couldn't possibly miss it. The
red index card clipped to it was marked "Jan. 24—5:00
p.m.; Jan 25—7:00 a.m." The time referred to the feeding schedule, and Lyn was glad to see she need only make
one trip today, although the 7:00 a.m. feeding tomorrow
morning dismayed her.

She had come here to rest, to do nothing, to forget, if
she could, what she had left behind in Philadelphia. Despite her cheerful reassurances to Pat, she didn't really
want to work. She could only hope that Casey Carmichael would be the last of Pat's clients to make an impulsive out-of-town trip.

It took half an hour to pet, comb and feed the
Greshams' cats, and to walk Mr. Jolly's basset hound.
Lyn was home by eight forty-five, and napping on the
sofa by nine o'clock. She awoke in time for lunch, and
took a magazine out onto the pool patio. She had barely
read a page, however, before the soporific effects of sun
and humidity took over, and she stretched out in the
lounge chair and dozed.

Lyn's long naps had been another matter of constant
concern for Pat, who considered that kind of lethargy an
unhealthy sign of deeper problems. Under other circumstances, Lyn would have been the first to agree with her.
But her sister did not know about the nightmares that

woke Lyn in the middle of the night and left her drenched
in a cold sweat, afraid to close her eyes again yet just as
afraid to lie awake in the dark with the memories. Nights
left her exhausted, and the days of pretending to Pat that
she was doing fine left her drained. Lyn was aware
enough to know that sleep was an escape, not a solution, but escape was exactly what she had come to Florida to do.

It was after five when she awoke, stretched out her
cramped legs and, blinking in the setting sun, remembered the three sets of pets that were waiting to be fed and
groomed. She groaned a little at the prospect. The first
two she didn't mind, but she was not looking forward to
the long drive into the country and the Carmichael
menagerie.

Lyn took care of the Greshams' cats and Mr. Jolly's
fish first, since they were on her way out of town. She
munched on a doughnut as she took the state road that
led to Casey Carmichael's place—her diet was another
thing she had given up on since leaving Philadelphia—
and arrived a little after six.

White post fencing lined the road and the driveway,
and she had to get out of the car to unfasten, then refas-
ten, a horse gate. All of this Pat's notebook had duti-
fully recorded. The long gravel driveway was dotted with
citrus trees, and several areas of the field on either side
were fenced off into sections with chain link, for what
purpose Lyn could not imagine. She passed three out-
buildings before she ever reached the neat, yellow-and-
white house and the gray barn that stood behind it. There
were several vehicles in the yard, among them a Winnebago, a van and a Jeep, so Lyn had to drive behind the
barn to park. She got out of the car, looking around her
in dismay.

Two collies and a large golden retriever came bounding up to meet her. Two roan horses grazed near the barn and three sheep pressed their dusty bodies against the rails of another fence, looking at her soulfully. She could hear the clatter and squawk of a nearby chicken coop, and a raucous clamor of barks and yips came from what could only be a kennel behind the house. A kennel! Obviously, she should have read Pat's notes more carefully.

She opened the door to recover the notebook and the golden retriever promptly leaped into the front seat.

"Okay, girl—boy," she corrected on second glance, "come on, get out! That's a good boy, come on!" The dog panted at her happily.

She picked up the notebook and flipped through it until she found a page that described a "Golden Retriever, male." "Montana," she said, looking at the retriever. "And you guys," she glanced behind her at the two collies, who sat alertly at her heels, "must be Riff and Raff. Well, you all look like good dogs but I'm running behind schedule here. Come on, Montana, let's go! Out of the car, boy!"

Montana snatched the notebook from her hand and shot past her in a flash.

"Hey!" she cried.

She took one step after him and promptly tripped over Riff or Raff, both of whom were now lying, as though on command, directly in her path. She picked herself up and dusted off her hands, searching for the errant retriever. The two collies watched her expectantly. "Montana!" she called in her sternest voice. "You come back here you bad dog!" And then, wheedling, "Here, Montana! Where'd you go, boy?"

Then she saw him, peeking out from behind the corner of the house, her notebook still clenched in his teeth.

She took off at a run. The collies circled her, barking noisily, obviously enjoying the opportunity to exercise their herding instincts. Lyn circled the house twice, with Montana always staying just out of reach and the collies leaping and barking with her every step. When she reached the back steps for the third time Montana was sitting there waiting for her, the notebook placed, like bait in a trap, on the top step.

Lyn edged close to the dog until she was sure he wasn't going to snatch the book and run again, but he only watched her with an interested glint in his eye and what looked very much like a mischievous grin on his face. Lyn snatched up the notebook at the first opportunity and glared at the dog, breathing hard. "And to think," she muttered, "I used to be an animal lover."

She wiped the notebook on the back of her jeans and pushed the damp tangle of pale red hair away from her forehead. She was hot and sweaty and had a stitch in her side, and she hadn't even begun to shovel hay and dish out kibble. She wondered whether or not it had ever occurred to Pat that there were easier ways to make a living.

She decided to take it one step at a time, according to Pat's directions and in the order they were given. The care of the horses and the sheep, to Lyn's immense relief, did not require that she pick up a shovel; she measured out their feed carefully and freshened their water with a garden hose. Likewise, the chickens required no hands-on attention. She stood outside the coop and scattered their feed on the ground through the chicken wire.

The kennel was actually a roomy fenced-off area containing half a dozen dogs of varying breeds and sizes, separate doghouses, and a central play area that was furnished with ramps for the dogs to climb on, old tires for them to chew on, and a multitude of mangled dog toys scattered around. Lyn entered carefully and was promptly mauled by dozens of muddy paws and wet tongues; she had to fight her way out again, slamming the gate and leaning against it hard.

The truth was, Lynn was not very experienced with animals and had never been a passionate dog lover. She and Pat had had pets as children, of course, but as she grew up she had become far too involved with the problems of the human race to have much time left over for the furry kingdom. A nice quiet cat or a goldfish she could deal with, but in the midst of this menagerie Lyn was completely out of her depth. Why, she wondered, hadn't she considered that *before* she volunteered to take over the pet-sitting business?

Her three canine escorts—the collies and the golden retriever—sat looking up at her curiously, and she returned their gaze with a dour twist of her lips. "So you could do better?" she challenged them.

Then she was disgusted with herself. This wasn't brain surgery, after all. She took a deep breath, braced herself for the onslaught, and edged her way back into the run, singing softly under her breath. Her voice was husky and not very good, but she had heard somewhere that music had a calming effect on animals and in this case it seemed to work—at least for the first five or ten seconds, until the novelty wore off. At that point the dogs descended on her again and she didn't have the time or the breath for singing. She filled the oversize washtub with fresh water as quickly as possible, managing to soak herself and three of the dogs in the process, and gathered up six food dishes, realizing only too late that it would have been easier to bring the dog food to the dishes than vice versa. It took three trips back and forth to the barn, where the food was stored, and by the time she finished she felt as though she had been through a war. She was covered with mud and dog hair, her face was streaked with grime, and if she spent the rest of the day in the shower she was sure she would never get the smell of dog out of her hair.

And she had yet to enter the house where, according to Pat, there were three litter trays to empty and Grizabella, Captain Ahab, Mr. Spock and Sasparilla to meet, among others.

"There ought to be a law," she grumbled, digging the house key out of her pocket.

She filled extra dishes for the collies and the retriever, and while they were eating she slipped inside the house. Despite the unfavorable impression she was beginning to form of the man who owned it, she did like his house. In contrast to the clean, uncluttered lines of Pat's home, this house looked as though it had been put together on a whim. None of the furniture matched, none of the floors was carpeted, none of the artwork was centered. The air was scented with a delicate, springtime fragrance that obviously came from an automatic air freshener—anyone who owned as many pets as this man would naturally find use for such a device—and Lyn gradually identified the perfume as that of fresh hyacinths. A delighted, slightly bemused grin spread over her face as she wondered what kind of man would choose to scent his home with hyacinths.

The rich green foliage of living plants and trees occupied every available space, giving a jungle impression. There were several carpeted cat posts and platforms scattered throughout, and a huge red-and-green parrot sat on a perch in the center of the room.

"Hello, bird," Lyn greeted him.

The parrot returned politely, "Hello."

She chuckled, and set out to discover the kitchen, where rations for the indoor pets were stored. On her way she passed through what might have once been a dining room, but had now been converted into a menagerie of a different sort. There were three floor-to-ceiling wire cages, each complete with platform scratching posts, litter trays, beds, and cats. Lyn counted seven altogether, most of them in pairs—two chocolate point Siamese, two white shorthair, two black longhair... and Grizabella.

Grizabella rated a cage all her own, and Lyn could easily see why. She was the most gorgeous cat Lyn had ever seen, a silky haired calico Persian with amber eyes and gold and black markings that were as unusual as they were somehow familiar to Lyn. Her name was inscribed in flowing script on a brass plate attached to the cage door, and purple velvet curtains were held back with gold tassels. Grizabella herself sat on a miniature velvet hassock, grooming herself and regarding Lyn with cool disdain.

"Wow," Lyn said. "Talk about overindulging your pets..."

But as she came closer, she began to understand why a little indulgence might be considered appropriate... and why it was that Grizabella looked so familiar. The food and water dishes on the cage floor were silver plated and inscribed with the name of Saucy Paws cat food. On a shelf parallel to the cage were several trophies, the first of which was the shape of a crown, and was inscribed, "In appreciation to Grizabella the Wonder Cat for three years' service, from Saucy Paws Cat Food."

Grizabella, the Saucy Paws cat. She was a star!

Lyn regarded the cat with new respect, more impressed than she liked to admit. She had read somewhere that animal stars made as much as half a million a year, and she had never been this close to anyone—animal or human—who had that kind of earning power.

"Well, what do you know about that?" Lyn unfastened the latch of the cage and reached inside, stroking the cat softly. "One day I'm a lowly social worker from Philadelphia, the next I'm brushing out the coat of the most famous cat in America. Is this a great country, or what?"

She laughed softly as Grizabella turned to lick her stroking fingers, and she was absolutely unprepared for what happened next. Grizabella suddenly stopped licking and clamped down hard with her sharp pointed teeth. Lyn screeched with pain and jerked her hand away; the parrot squawked and launched itself from its perch to Lyn's hair, digging its talons into her scalp; a dog started to bark, loudly and quite close. And all of this was almost simultaneous. Lyn whirled around with a squeal of alarm and pain, trying to dislodge the parrot, tripped over Montana, who had somehow gotten in through the door Lyn was almost certain she had closed behind her, and she cried out in dismay as Grizabella launched herself from her cage and dashed past her. Lyn threw out her arms to block the cat but missed by a wide margin. She watched helplessly as half a million dollars worth of feline scampered down the hallway and out of sight.

For almost a full minute Lyn stood there, dumbfounded, openmouthed and staring. The parrot squawked again, disengaged its claws from her hair, and fluttered out of the room. Montana gave one last delighted bark and charged down the hall in the direction the cat had gone.

Galvanized into action, Lyn stumbled after the dog and arrived in the kitchen just in time to see Montana wriggle through a dog door, leaving it flapping on its hinges. Lyn stared at the small door in dismay.

"No," she said out loud. "The cat did not go through the dog door. Please, don't let the cat have gone through the dog door. . . ."

She couldn't believe this had happened. The day had started out so well. She had done nothing to deserve this, she hadn't even asked for this job, all she had ever wanted was to be left alone to nap by the pool. She was just doing her sister a favor: feed a few animals, brush a few coats . . . how hard could it be? But within the past half hour she had been mauled by dogs, attacked by a parrot, and now Grizabella the Wonder Cat, star of television, magazines, and cat food boxes all over the country, had escaped into the night.

No. She took a deep breath, and convinced herself silently again. *No*. The cat could not have gone outside, she simply couldn't have. It was dark outside, there were dozens of trees to climb and bushes to hide in and Lyn would never find her if she was outside. Therefore, the cat must be hiding somewhere in the house.

Lyn began a hopeful chorus of "Here, Kitty, Kitty" as she circled through the house. She opened cabinets, she looked under tables, she crawled behind draperies and under furniture. She wondered if Casey Carmichael had insurance. She wondered if *Pat* had insurance.

"Grizabella. . ." she called in her softest, most inviting voice as she started up the stairs. "Here, kitty, kitty... Where are you, you stupid cat?"

And suddenly she stopped, frozen in place, as a sound reached her that she had been too preoccupied to notice before. It was the sound of water running, coming from behind a closed door at the top of the stairs. Someone was in the house. She was not alone.

Panic slammed through her for a brief instant and the first thing she thought was *burglar!* She gripped the rail and had taken two running steps down the stairs before common sense reasserted itself and she stopped, taking another deep breath. The back door had been locked, hadn't it? The house hadn't appeared to be ransacked. And what kind of burglar would break in just to take a shower?

Maybe the owner had returned early. Or maybe it *was* a burglar with fastidious habits. She almost preferred the latter to having Casey Carmichael discover her here, and Grizabella missing.

Her cowardly instincts demanded that she leave the house with all possible speed, but as she glanced back up the stairs something caught her eye. A door was partly open on the left side of the hall, across from what she assumed to be the bathroom. The half-open door would be an irresistible invitation to an errant cat, and if there was a chance, any chance at all, that she could catch Grizabella and return her to her cage before she was discovered here...

On tiptoe, she hurried up the remaining stairs, glancing worriedly over her shoulder where the sound of running water continued from the bathroom, and peeked behind the open door. It was a walk-in closet. The shelves on either side were filled with towels and cleaning supplies, but no cat was to be found.

Sick with disappointment, she turned around. And she screamed.

Directly opposite her was the biggest, most ferocious-looking feline Lyn had ever seen outside a zoo. Ears flattened, muscles tensed in a crouch, it must have outweighed Lyn by a hundred pounds. She couldn't make another sound. She couldn't even draw a breath. And she only had time to take one stumbling step back into the closet before the creature roared, and prepared to spring.

Two

"Sheba! Cut!"

It was perhaps five seconds after the strong male voice sliced across her consciousness before Lyn was able to open her eyes. Even then she was not entirely sure she believed what she saw. One moment she had been staring into the jaws of death, and the next into a pair of angry green eyes—accompanied by a water-slick male body that was, as far as Lyn could tell, completely naked.

Somewhat belatedly, all things considered, Lyn's knees buckled beneath her and she slid to the closet floor, expelling the breath from her lungs in a single gasp. She couldn't take her eyes off the man—or more accurately, off the big feline that shielded her view of him from waist to knee. The cat's smooth, tawny coat gleamed, its muscles twitched, its tail swung slowly back and forth. Its eyes regarded Lyn warily, and another low rumble issued from its throat.

"Sheba!" the man said sharply. "I said shut up!"

The huge cat gave Lyn one last resentful look, swished its tail haughtily, and sauntered away, moving down the stairs. Lyn's heart started beating again with hammering rush.

The man advanced on her, scowling, and Lyn realized her relief might have been premature. "Who the hell are you," he demanded, "and what are you doing in my house?"

He was not, after all, completely naked, but for the scantiness of the somewhat less-than-standard-size black bath towel he had wrapped around his waist he might as well have been. Bare feet, strong-boned ankles, and lean calves moved into her line of vision. Damp footprints scarred the hardwood floor, and as she watched a bead of water slid from his knee and trailed into the light pattern of smooth brown hair that textured his legs. She forced her eyes upward, over the scrap of towel that clung low on his hips, and picked up the triangle of water-straight hair where it formed a V over his navel and flared upward across his lean, surprisingly taut-muscled chest. His throat showed a flush of anger—or perhaps it was simply the heat from the shower—and a froth of shaving soap still clung to his jaw. His wet hair molded his scalp but showed a resistant little curl just below his ear; its color could have been anything from dark blond to brown. His eyes were very green, and very fiery.

And with all of this to contend with, Lyn was proud of the presence of mind it took to demand, "Who are *you*?"

"I live here!" he shot back. "You've got a lot of explaining to do, lady, and you'd better do it fast before I lose my sense of humor and call Sheba back."

He was standing on the threshold of the closet now, pinning her in. Lyn pushed herself to her feet, galvanized by the mere mention of the giant cat's name. "That animal could have killed me!" she cried. "Are you crazy? What kind of person keeps a—a *lion* in his house?"

He regarded her coolly. "The kind of person who values the safety of his home. And she's not a lion," he added. "She's a cougar. Are you going to answer my question now, or shall we wait for the police?"

"Police?" she gasped. "Police!" After all she had been through, that was the final straw. "*I'm* the one who should call the police! For—for fraud and assault and battery and running a zoo without a license! And concealing a deadly weapon! I'm *supposed* to be here! I was *hired* to be here! And I still don't know who you are—you say you live here but you could be some crazy person who likes to break into houses with a lion—cougar—and make himself at home while the owner is away. The world is full of perverts." She was babbling now, a sign of severe stress and emotional exhaustion she was sure, compounded by the fact that he had taken a step inside the closet and was completely blocking her exit. "Let me by!"

He made no move. "What do you mean you were hired? Who hired you?"

"The *owner* did! I'm the pet sitter!"

"Don't give me that. You—" And then he stopped, and looked at her more closely. "You're Pat's sister?"

He was so close that she could smell the steamy scent of his soap, and feel the humid warmth of his body. She tried to push past him. "Get out of my way. Let me by."

"Wait a minute." His face hardened into suspicion again. "You were supposed to be here at five. If you *are* the sitter, you should have come and gone by now."

"And you're supposed to be out of town! Will you get out of my way?"

"I called and left a message—"

"I didn't get any message!"

Lyn's nerves had been strung to a fine point long before ever venturing up the stairs; the encounter with the cougar had not helped any, and though Casey Carmichael—if that was indeed, who he was—was probably well within his rights, his unexpected appearance and blatant threats had managed to turn a mildly disastrous evening into a full-blown catastrophe. She didn't want to deal with this. No one had *told* her she would have to deal with this. She just wanted to go home and put this entire debacle behind her.

And, naturally, Montana the mischievous retriever chose that moment to come bounding up the stairs and join them in the closet.

He pushed into the narrow opening with wagging tail and panting tongue, his wriggling body unbalancing them both so that, before she knew it, Lyn was falling against a bare male chest, her feet tangled between a pair of unclothed male legs. She tried to disengage herself, but that was easier said than done, with a man on one side and a dog on the other, both of them appearing to do their best to knock her off her feet.

"Let me go!" she cried, struggling to pull away from his hands on her shoulders. "Call off your crazy dog!" She lurched backward, but he was jostled forward at the same moment, pinning her against the back wall.

He yelped as she stepped on his foot trying to regain her balance. "Watch it!"

"*You* watch it!" She gasped as his hand brushed her breast. "I'm not kidding! You get away from me right now or I'll—"

"Will you stop—Montana, get out of here! Ow!" he exclaimed as her foot made contact with his bare toe again.

"I'll do worse than that if you don't—"

"Montana, go!" he commanded the dog with an abrupt gesture of his wrist.

Montana looked at him alertly, then turned and left the closet.

"Now." He stepped away from her, cautiously releasing her shoulders. "Before this gets out of hand—"

"It already *is* out of hand!" Lyn replied haughtily and started to push past him once again.

Before she could stop it, before, in fact, she even realized what was happening, the closet door started to swing toward her. It closed with a snap and plunged them into blackness.

Lyn uttered an inarticulate sound and plunged toward the door, searching for the knob.

"Montana!" he declared with soft venom. And then, somewhat apologetically he added, "He's been taught to close doors behind him."

Lyn bent over, running her hands up and down the smooth wood paneling. "I can't find the doorknob!"

"Move over." He took her place, searching for a moment, and then stepped away. "There's a good reason for that," he informed her. "There isn't one."

Only a thin stream of the hall light penetrated the closet, and he was nothing more than a shadow in the dark. Still, she stared at him as though actually expecting to discern some sign of humor on his face. "You are kidding." Her voice was flat, then began to rise with incredulity and denial. "What do you mean there's no doorknob? What kind of house doesn't have *doorknobs?*"

"Whoever heard of putting doorknobs on the inside of closets? It's not like I planned on getting locked into one!"

"Well—do something! Take the door off the hinges, jimmy the latch—something!"

His voice was dry. "I seem to have left my tools in my pants, which don't happen to be hanging up in here."

Lyn released a long breath through her teeth. "I don't believe this. So what are we supposed to do? Just stay here until they find our bodies?"

"I doubt it'll come to that." His voice was a little too cheerful for Lyn's liking. "If I don't make my house payment by the first of the month, they'll send out the loan sharks, and they can be counted on to tear this place apart until they find me."

"That's very funny." Lyn braced her back to the wall and slid down to the floor, folding her arms atop her upraised knees. "I don't believe this," she muttered into her arms. "I just don't believe this. . . ."

His silence could have been interpreted as apology, or amusement. Then he said, "This seems like a good time to introduce ourselves."

She raised her eyes to him again in disbelief and amazement, and once again could make out nothing but the shadow of a form.

"I'm Kevin Carmichael," he said. "Most people call me Casey."

His casual, cocktail-party tone left her speechless for a moment. Then she said, "Why?"

"K.C.," he explained patiently. "Casey."

"Oh."

"And your name?"

"Lyn Sanders."

"Pleased to meet you."

He surprised her by sitting on the floor next to her, so close that his knee brushed against her jeaned thigh. Quickly she jerked away. "What are you doing?"

"Making myself comfortable."

She pressed farther against the far wall. "Can't you make yourself comfortable somewhere else?"

"Are you always this jumpy?"

"Sorry." She tried to make her voice light, but it came out as strained and tense. "There's something about being trapped in a closet with a naked man in a strange house with no chance of rescue that puts my nerves on edge."

His voice was rich with amusement. "You can relax. I'm not feeling particularly lusty at the moment, and even if I were there's not enough room in here to do anything about it."

He was right about that, at least. Though Lyn had pressed herself so far against the wall that a shelf dug uncomfortably into her ribs, the damp warmth of his lean bicep still brushed against hers and she could feel the shape of his hip—protected only by the scrap of towel—curving against her thigh. The shower-fresh scent of him filled the small enclosure.

He said, "Now, let's see if we can't get this thing straightened out. Do you still think I'm a burglar with a shower fetish, or do you believe I'm who I say I am?"

Lyn doubled her fists atop her knees and rested her chin on them morosely, trying to ignore the flexing of his thigh muscle as he shifted position slightly. "Oh, you're Casey Carmichael all right. According to Murphy's law you couldn't be anyone else."

"Murphy's Law?" There was a hint of puzzlement in his tone. "Which one?"

"The one that says 'anything that can go wrong, will go wrong,'" she answered, sighing. "Besides, you knew the dog's name."

He seemed to think about that for a minute—or perhaps he was just phrasing his next line of attack. "You don't look much like Pat," he pointed out.

"So I've been told."

"And you *are* two hours late."

"I overslept."

"Until five o'clock in the afternoon?"

"Five-thirty."

He was silent for a moment. "Do you have the key?"

"What?"

"The key to my house that Pat keeps on file."

Feeling both foolish and irritated that she hadn't thought of so simple a solution to proving her innocence, Lyn dug into her jeans pocket and produced the key.

Casey Carmichael's warm callused fingers fumbled with hers for a moment as he retrieved the key, then held it so that it struck the narrow wedge of light coming from beneath the door, examining the white tag with the familiar Pet Pride logo—a cartoon dog and cat etched in green—that was suspended from the chain. Satisfied, he returned the key to her.

"To tell the truth," he admitted easily, "it was pretty obvious you were the pet sitter from the start. I don't think a burglar could make up a story like that on the spur-of-the-moment."

Lyn scowled as she returned the key to her pocket. "I appreciate your vote of confidence. So you put me through all this just for the fun of it?"

Again there was that curve of amusement in his tone, making Lyn wonder what his smile looked like, and making her sorry she couldn't see it in the dark. "Do you mean you haven't been having fun?"

"Oh, sure. This is the best time I've had in years. Why go to the amusement park when you can be mauled by a parrot, attacked by a cougar and locked in a dark closet by a dog—and all without crossing the county line."

"Sheba wouldn't have hurt you, you know. She's been declawed, and she's really just a big pussycat."

"There was no cougar on your list of pets," Lyn pointed out darkly.

"That's because she's not officially mine. I only board her when we're working together. And I'd never leave her home with a sitter."

"Wise decision," Lyn muttered. Then, for the first time something besides her own miserable predicament prickled her interest and she asked, "What do you mean—working together?"

"That's what I do," he explained, "I train animals— for films and television commercials, mostly. That's where I was today—on a shoot."

"Oh," Lyn said. That certainly explained a lot…more than enough, as far as Lyn was concerned. That meant he was not only Grizabella's owner, but her trainer as well, and losing the cat was more than just the cost of a calico Persian. It was his livelihood. She felt a little sick.

There was an accusatory note in her tone as she pointed out, "You were supposed to be gone overnight. Pat's note distinctly said—"

The shrug of his shoulders against hers was like a caress. "We had to reschedule. If you've ever tried to share a Winnebago with a two-hundred-pound cat who likes to hog the bed, you'll understand why I decided to drive back tonight instead of in the morning."

Lyn could feel his grin in the dark as he added, "And as it turns out I'm having a much more interesting evening than I would have if I'd stayed over. Sometimes it pays to go with your impulses."

"You must lead a dull life if you call this an interesting way to spend an evening."

"You make the most out of what you've got."

"And what, exactly, have I got—besides a hard floor and a closetful of towels?"

"A charming, articulate companion who is going out of his way to be pleasant despite the fact that none of this would have happened if it weren't for you."

Lyn knew she had absolutely no reason to be insulted, but she couldn't help it: the cumulative pressures of the day, the dark guilt over Grizabella, and the close confinement with this sexy-smelling stranger combined into defensiveness and she snapped, "You're the one who pushed me into the closet—*and* set his attack cat on me."

"You're the one who was two hours late."

"You're the one who called a pet sitter in the first place—and came home before you were supposed to! And while we're on the subject you've got a lot of nerve asking Pat to take care of twenty-seven animals for a lousy ten dollars a visit."

"I couldn't help that—my kennel boy called in sick at the last minute." His voice was mild and perfectly reasonable. "Besides, we have an arrangement. Naturally I pay her more than the usual rate. Did anybody ever mention that you have a sour disposition?"

She hesitated. "I'm sorry," she said, and meant it. "I'm usually a nice person—really. People like me. I mean, people are always saying how much fun I am— well, maybe not fun, but at least, well, nice. I really don't mean to take it out on you, you've been very understanding all things considered—it's just that I've had a really rotten day. Or afternoon.''

She released a long breath and propped her hands on her chin again. "Besides," she added with more reluctance than she had ever felt in her life. "I have something else to tell you.''

"Oh?"

"I lost your cat.''

"Which cat?"

She felt her muscles tense, one by one, from toes to fingers. But there was no point in putting it off any longer. "Grizabella. The Wonder Cat.''

He was silent for a long, long time.

She blurted out, "I didn't mean to—I had to open the cage to feed her, didn't I? I was just petting her, and all of a sudden she bit me! Then the parrot—and the dog... I've looked everywhere, I swear I have, but the dog door was open and . . . well, I'm afraid she might have gotten outside.''

Again the silence, long and agonizing. And just when Lyn thought she couldn't stand it for another moment he said, "Let's get back to the part about your being trapped in a closet with a naked man. As far as the conversation goes, that had possibilities.''

She stared at him. "Did you hear what I said? I lost Grizabella.''

The silence was a little briefer, and somewhat less ominous this time. "There's not much either of us can do about it from in here, is there?''

Lyn swallowed hard. "I guess she was—valuable.''

"Irreplaceable.''

The cold lump of dread that had formed in Lyn's throat settled to her stomach. She buried her face in her knees. "Oh, God. I'm sorry... You'd think that I could manage to feed a few animals without causing a major disaster, wouldn't you? I mean, a ten-year-old could do this job! Maybe you would have been better off hiring a ten-year-old. Here I am, a grown woman, college educated, fairly knowledgeable in the ways of the world—and I can't do even the simplest thing right. I'm sorry," she repeated miserably.

"There, there." Without warning, his arm slipped around her shoulders in a friendly, reassuring gesture, and if Lyn hadn't known better she would have sworn there was an undertone of humor in his voice. "Try not to let this scar you permanently."

She lifted her face, half suspicious, half relieved. "You don't seem very upset."

"I don't see any point in making you feel worse than you already do."

Lyn swallowed hard. She was acutely aware of his arm around her shoulders, its warmth and firm shape drawing her into an embrace that was more intimate in the dark than it would have been otherwise. She knew she should probably make some effort to shift away, but she did not. The truth was, there was something rather pleasant about the atmosphere between them now, and she did not want to spoil it just yet.

She said, "Thank you. That's very generous of you. I know how you must feel, losing a famous cat like that."

"Actually, I never liked her much. She's a biter, and temperamental as hell."

Lyn stared at him in openmouthed astonishment for a moment, then quickly decided she'd better quit while she was ahead. She said instead, somewhat uncertainly, "You certainly are an even-tempered man."

"In my line of work, you have to be."

"I suppose so."

She was growing uncomfortable now. His nearness, his clean masculine scent, reminded her that her clothes were muddy, her hair was tangled, and she smelled like dogs. Moreover, now that the worst was over and she had confessed about Grizabella, she was becoming more and more aware of how provocative their positions were—how firm the shape of his leg was against hers, how secure the cradle of his arm. When she considered the fact that this was only the beginning of a very long night she felt a flush spread over her throat and down to the tips of her fingers.

She cleared her throat abruptly and said, "It's getting warm in here, isn't it?"

"Is it? I was just thinking it's a little chilly."

"That might have something to do with the way you're dressed."

He chuckled. "It might, at that."

She pushed to her feet quickly, finding it necessary to brace her hand briefly against his bare knee but trying to make the movement as casual as possible. "Are you sure there's nothing in here we can use to open the door? There has to be something . . ." She ran her hands along the shelves, dislodging towels, fumbling over canisters and bottles. As a stack of washcloths scattered off the shelf and onto Casey's head, he very prudently got to his feet.

"Look, there's nothing in here." He caught both of her searching hands with his. "I know my own closet."

"You didn't know it didn't have doorknobs." She gave an experimental little tug to retrieve her hands, but not very hard. Her eyes had adjusted to the dimness enough so that she could see his face only a few inches above hers, and his breath was a warm whisper on her cheek when he spoke.

"But I know there aren't any tools in here."

She pulled her hands away. "Are you going to sue me for losing Grizabella?"

"Not if you don't sue me."

"Sue you?" She blinked. "For what?"

He shrugged, leaning back so that one hip rested casually against a shelf. "People do. The postman who was scared by a bear, the cleaning lady who stumbled over a python..."

"Python?" Her voice squeaked.

"Don't worry," he assured her. "I don't keep snakes anymore. But the point is, you never can tell how people are going to react when they have a bad experience with an exotic animal."

"I wouldn't know. This is my first experience with exotic animals and I'm too embarrassed to sue."

She could see his smile filtering faintly through the dark. "That's a relief. Now that we've got the confusion about mistaken identities cleared up and we've promised not to sue each other, do you think we could be friends?"

Lyn's own smile came more easily than she ever could have imagined a half hour ago. "I don't see why not." She extended her hand to him.

"Good." He took her hand in a brief, warm clasp, then turned toward the door. "Montana! Open!"

Outside she heard the scuffling of paws, an eager panting, and the definitive click of a latch. She watched in disbelief as the crack of light widened and the closet door swung slowly open.

"Good dog."

Montana sat just outside the door, looking very pleased with himself, and Casey stepped outside to scratch him under the chin. For a moment Lyn simply stared at them both, unmoving, and then she burst out,

"How did he— You—you knew, all along you knew—and you—you *told* him to—"

Casey looked at her patiently. "No, I didn't command him to close the door. I told you, he does that on his own. But as long as we were in there, it seemed like a good chance to get things cleared up—"

"You kept me trapped in there!"

"Well, I couldn't let you go storming off the way you were, could I? There's no telling what you might do."

She glared at him. "Like sue you?"

His smile, now that she could see it, was even more disarming than she had imagined it would be. His full lips curved upward, his eyes narrowed with a warm glow, and his entire face took on a mischievous, all but irresistibly endearing look. "You promised," he reminded her.

Lyn pushed past him toward the stairs—and almost tripped over Grizabella, who came strolling down the hallway with her tail in the air.

"Well, look at that," Casey declared, and bent to scoop her up. "She's not lost after all."

Lyn turned on him icily. "I suppose you knew *that*, too."

He lifted one shoulder innocently. "She gets out all the time. Usually she ends up hiding in my underwear drawer—she's too big a coward to go outside."

Lyn didn't know whether to be furious or relieved; whether to count her blessings or kick Casey Carmichael in the shins. What she did know was that if she stayed here one moment longer she would be certain to do something she regretted.

So she drew back her shoulders, squared her jaw, and said, with all possible dignity, "Thank you, Mr. Carmichael, for a perfectly enchanting evening."

She turned and stalked down the stairs.

There was laughter in his voice as he called back, "Hey, don't go away mad!"

Lyn slammed the door behind her.

Three

Lyn had not even disappeared down the stairs before Casey was wishing he had never taught Montana to open doors. Why had Pat never told him how attractive her sister was? And not just attractive, the way Pat was, although Casey had always had a weakness for redheads, but...compelling. Yes, that was the word. Interesting in a way that made him want to know more about her. He couldn't help wondering what would have happened if they had stayed in that closet a little while longer.

But he was always doing things like that. Backing away prematurely, closing—or opening—doors too soon. That way he was never disappointed by what might have been, he was never the one left standing behind while the other person walked away. If he missed a lot in the process...well, he couldn't regret what he had never lost. And he had found that, when it came to dealing with the human race, a healthy dose of caution was a good policy.

But this time he didn't see how it could have hurt to get to know Lyn Sanders a little better.

He took Grizabella back into his bedroom while he quickly dressed and then went about the business of closing down the zoo for the night. Sheba followed him docilely to the garage, where her bed, made of a well-worn mattress and a couple of chewed-up blankets, lay in one corner. The cats howled with hungry demand when they heard his footsteps, the parrot circled the room and squawked excitedly. That was one thing about animals; they were always predictable.

He could, of course, call Lyn. It wasn't as though they were necessarily ships that passed in the night; he knew her number, he knew where she lived, he even knew her sister. If he wanted to see her again, all he had to do was pick up the phone.

But almost as soon as the notion crossed his mind he dismissed it. He didn't have time for a social life. He didn't have room in his life for another person. The last thing he needed was to get involved with a woman who, even on such brief acquaintance, he found far too attractive. He wasn't going to call her.

But, if he had it all to do over again, he decided he would have found a way to make her stay a little longer.

All the way to the car Lyn expected the giant cat to appear, teeth bared, or one of the dogs to leap out from behind a bush and knock her to the ground, or the parrot to fly out of an open window and land in her hair. She walked with rapid, though cautious, steps, her eyes darting back and forth between the shadows, and when she reached her car without incident she felt like a prisoner on reprieve. She could hardly believe it had been that easy.

And as it turned out, of course, it wasn't that easy. Nothing ever was. She lifted the door handle, and nothing happened. The door was locked. She could see her purse on the front seat of the car. Desperately, she patted the pockets of her jeans. No keys. With a sinking feeling, she peered through the window on the driver's side and, sure enough, there were her keys, dangling from the ignition.

"No," she groaned. "Please, no..."

She hurried around to the passenger side and tried the door, knowing it was futile. The door locks were automatic; if one was locked, all of them were. How could she have been so stupid?

But she *wasn't* that stupid. If that dog hadn't jumped in her car and stolen her notebook, she never would have locked her keys inside. Now she was stuck in the last place in the world she wanted to be; she was tired, she was dirty, she was hungry, and it was all Casey Carmichael's fault.

Angrily she kicked at a tire, but missed and banged her ankle against the fender. She smothered a yelp of pain and grabbed her ankle, overbalanced, and almost fell. Righting herself, she took a couple of breaths and glared at the car.

It was clear she had two choices. She could either break a window to get into her own car, or go back to the house, knock meekly on Casey Carmichael's door, and ask for assistance. She seriously considered breaking a window.

Almost wincing with dread, she looked back at the house. The kitchen window painted a bright square of yellow against the early-winter night, and she caught a glimpse of a shadow moving back and forth in front of it. In the kennel, the dogs who had begun to bark when they heard her approach settled down. She wondered uneasily where Sheba the cougar was.

Of course, she tried to rationalize, it wasn't really Casey Carmichael's fault that she'd locked her keys in the car. And he hadn't *really* ordered the dog to lock them in the closet together. Although there was no getting past the fact that he had certainly taken advantage of the situation, he had for the most part been a perfect gentleman and even rather pleasant. Toward the end, she had almost begun to like him. Perhaps she had overreacted.

But how was she going to go back to that house and politely knock on the door after slamming out so angrily? Her dramatic exit would be spoiled, at the very least. At the worst, Casey Carmichael would laugh so hard he'd forget to let her in.

Well, he would just have to laugh. The temperature was dropping and gooseflesh was beginning to rise on her bare arms. And she couldn't find a rock big enough to break the window with.

She went to the house, knocked timidly on the back door, and when no one answered, she pounded. He took his time responding, and a trace of annoyance returned. However, when she heard the click of a latch and the door slowly swung open, Lyn deliberately smoothed her features and prepared to be polite. She even managed a small smile as she opened her mouth to speak, and then stopped. There was no one there.

She looked into a yellow kitchen, comfortably cluttered like the rest of his house, but completely devoid of human habitation. She dropped her eyes and found, as she should have expected, Montana sitting before the open door.

Her mouth dropped wryly. "Is your master home?" she inquired.

Montana's bark was short and to the point.

"Hi." Casey Carmichael came around the corner, a bag of cat food under one arm and a Siamese cat under the other. He did not look particularly surprised to see her. "Did you forget something?"

He had, Lyn was relieved to see, changed his attire since the last time they had met. He was wearing red running shorts that didn't cover much more than the towel had done, and a black-and-white T-shirt. His hair had dried into tousled, sun-bleached waves that were pushed back from his forehead and curled softly against his neck. In the full light of the kitchen, more or less clothed and dry, he was even sexier than Lyn had imagined him to be in the closet.

She cleared her throat and made a vague gesture behind her, not stepping over the threshold. "Actually, I wondered if I could use your phone. I need to call the auto club."

The cat yowled, and Casey allowed it to jump to the floor, casting an inquiring look at Lyn. "Car trouble?"

"In a way." She felt an uncomfortable flush tickle her cheeks. If he laughed... "I—seem to have locked my keys in the car."

The grin that tugged at Casey's lips was not mirth, but something very close to delight. *If wishes were horses,* he thought. She stood framed by the doorway, her face framed by crinkly tendrils of humidity-laden red hair, her porcelain skin faintly stained with embarrassed color, her eyes stubbornly defiant. He was not sure he had ever met a woman who could look quite so good in faded jeans and a baggy white T-shirt streaked with muddy paw prints, but that was all part of her appeal. She looked as though she had been in the trenches, and here she was, a proud survivor, ready to do battle again.

He would not have called her, he was sure of that. But he was glad she had come back.

He brought the grin under control, but could not entirely subdue the twinkle in his eyes. He didn't laugh. For that, Lyn would have forgiven him almost anything.

He said, "Why do I get the impression you're not a very organized person?"

Lyn started to inform him of the part Montana had played in this latest incident, but swallowed back the retort. She repeated, "Could I use the phone?"

His response was, "I don't suppose you got around to feeding the indoor animals."

She hesitated, torn between outrage over the suspicion that he was going to make her work for the privilege of using the phone, and guilt over the fact that she had not finished the job she was hired to do in the first place. Finally, chagrined, she admitted, "In all the confusion... No, I guess I didn't."

"I tell you what. Why don't you finish that while I make myself some supper, then I'll see what I can do about your car."

That was certainly a fair proposition, but still Lyn hesitated. She looked around uneasily. "Where's Sheba?"

He flashed her a grin. "Bedded down for the night in the garage. And you don't have to worry about Grizabella, either. She's already been fed and brushed."

Lyn came inside and closed the door. She knew she should probably leave well enough alone, but she had never been the kind of person to let disputes go unresolved. She said, "I'm sorry I lost my temper before. But

I still think what you did was wrong, and I don't like being manipulated."

He lifted a perfectly innocent eyebrow. "Is that what I did?"

"You know that's what you did." She tried to keep the shortness out of her voice. "And it was completely unnecessary."

He seemed unimpressed as he opened the refrigerator door. "It was for a good cause, wasn't it? The cat food is on the counter. I found your notebook beside Grizabella's cage, and all the feeding instructions are there."

For once, Lyn's better judgment prevailed, and she did not continue the argument. She picked up the bag of cat food and proceeded to do her job.

When she returned to the kitchen after the last water dish was filled, the smell of sizzling bacon made her mouth water. The only thing she had had since breakfast was a doughnut, and it was long past her suppertime.

Her longing expression must have given her away, because Casey glanced up from the peanut butter he was spreading on a slice of bread. "Have you eaten?"

"Well, I . . ."

"Here, there's plenty. Help yourself."

She watched dubiously as he added three slices of bacon to the peanut butter sandwich, but she was too hungry to be particular. "Well . . . Maybe I'll just have a snack."

Casey handed her the peanut-butter-coated knife and placed his own sandwich on a saucer. "Montana," he said, moving to the table. "Bring me a beer."

Lyn watched in amazement as Montana scampered eagerly across the linoleum, stepped on the foot pedal that opened the refrigerator, and poked his head inside. A moment later he backed away, a can of beer clenched in his teeth, jumped on the refrigerator door to close it, and walked proudly over to Casey.

Casey took the beer from the dog and scratched his ears. "Good boy. Go lie down."

"I don't believe it!" Lyn said, still staring at the dog. "That's the most incredible thing I've ever seen. How in the world did you teach him to do that?"

Casey wiped the can with the hem of his T-shirt before setting it down, then began to move piles of mail, newspapers, and other miscellanea off the kitchen table. "It's really one of the least complicated tricks you can teach. Just a sequence of behaviors that more or less come naturally...walking, retrieving, and jumping. Dogs are a lot like people in that respect: they'll do anything in the world for you, as long as it's what they wanted to do in the first place."

Lyn shook her head in amazement, and turned back to spreading peanut butter on her sandwich. However annoying and autocratic Casey Carmichael might be, she could not deny that he was very, very good at what he did—and what he did was fascinating. "Maybe," she agreed, "but I still think that's one smart dog."

"Average dog," Casey corrected, "brilliant trainer."

This time his grin was infectious, and Lyn shared it, though somewhat dryly. "I guess it helps that you don't suffer from ego problems."

"I can't afford to. The minute these animals started to suspect I was less than perfect, I'd be overrun by a giant revolt. And let's face it, smart as they are, I haven't met a dog or a cat yet who was qualified to negotiate a contract, so we're all better off if I stay in charge."

Lyn chuckled and placed her sandwich on a paper napkin. "I guess that's one way to look at it."

"What would you like to drink?"

Lyn had never considered herself a gourmand, but she didn't think even she could face beer with peanut butter. So she said, "I'm driving. Maybe milk?"

"Sorry, Montana can't manage that one. The glasses are in that cabinet over your head."

Lyn helped herself to a glass and milk, feeling more at ease than she ever would have thought possible in a stranger's kitchen. As she sat down across from Casey at the small table she said, "Is Montana a movie star, too?"

Casey took a bite of his sandwich and shook his head. When he had swallowed, he added, "He's done a few commercials, but mostly I use him for demonstrations and to help train other dogs. He started out in search-and-rescue, but was also one of the first service dogs I trained. That's why he has to be allowed some degree of independent thinking—and why he's not always very reliable before the cameras."

Lyn frowned a little as she tore the crusts off her bread with her fingers. "Service dog? What's that?"

"Handicapped assistance, mostly. I don't do as much of that as I used to, but every once in a while I'll get a dog that shows a real knack for it. There's nothing sadder than an unemployed dog, so I give them on-site training and send them off to profitable, fulfilling careers."

"Aren't any of your animals just pets?"

That was a question Casey had been asked many times over the course of his career. No one seemed to be able to understand why an animal as cute and cuddly as Grizabella, or as entertaining as Montana, should ever have to serve any other function. He answered, "There's nothing more useless, or pitiful, than a pet. Put yourself in the animal's place. Everybody needs a purpose in life."

Lyn said, "I don't know. Free room and board, all the attention you want, and no stress except a trip to the vet once or twice a year... I think I could deal with that."

"A vegetable has a more interesting life."

As far as Lyn was concerned, the life of a vegetable had certain appeal as well, but she didn't want to argue with him. So she commented instead, "It must be hard to raise an animal, grow attached to it, and then have to give it away."

He shrugged. "Not really. They do their job, I do mine. As long as I've been in this business, if I let myself get all worked up every time I lost an animal I'd be a real mess by now."

Casey was aware that that sounded a little cold, so he quickly changed the subject. "I get the impression pet sitting is not your usual line of work. Are you just helping Pat out part-time?"

Lyn's lips tightened in a self-conscious smile. "Gee, what gave me away?" Then she answered, "I've been staying with Pat for a couple of weeks, and I knew how much she needed this vacation. So I volunteered to look after the business while she was gone." She couldn't prevent a regretful little sigh as she added, "It sounded like a good idea at the time."

"So you're just visiting?"

Casey's eyes were alert and interested, and Lyn felt slightly uncomfortable beneath his gaze. She wished she had thought to straighten her hair while she was out of the room feeding the animals, or at least checked a mirror to see if her face was clean.

She pushed a frizzy tendril of hair behind her ear and answered, "I'm not really sure yet. I'm kind of on a leave of absence from my job in Philadelphia until I make up my mind what I want to do."

Another man might have been disappointed, but Casey was oddly relieved. Another man probably wouldn't have tried so hard to convince himself he did not find her nearly as interesting as he did, but knowing that there was no chance she could become a permanent fixture in his life made everything much easier. Almost imperceptibly, he felt himself relax.

"What did you do in Philadelphia?"

She answered briefly, "I was a social worker."

Perhaps it was the shortness of her reply that alerted him, or perhaps it was something on her face. His instincts for people were almost as sharp as they were for animals, and he knew there was more to the story than she was willing to tell. The quick clouding of pain in her gray eyes tugged at him, and there was something about the set of her mouth that seemed suddenly vulnerable. And he knew then that he did not want to know the rest of the story.

Lyn recognized the quiet thoughtfulness of his gaze and she tensed for an onslaught of prying questions. But he surprised her by replying only, "I can understand why you left. Give me a cage full of wild animals over the human jungle any day. So where did Pat go?"

The easy way in which he shifted the conversation to a more neutral subject was definitely a point in his favor as far as Lyn was concerned, and she was touched by his sensitivity. As a matter of fact, she decided there were quite a few things she liked about him—and still a great many she did not. He was arrogant and heavy-handed, supremely confident in himself and the rightness of his own thinking, and those were characteristics Lyn had never found admirable in anyone. On the other hand, he was good at light conversation and he didn't hold a grudge and he made her feel comfortable with him, which was no easy task. And he had the sexiest legs Lyn had seen on a man in a long time.

They talked about inconsequentials while they finished eating, and when Casey emptied the beer can and tossed it across the room into the trash bin, Lyn said, "I really should call the auto club. It'll probably take them a while to get here and—"

"Oh, I don't think there's any reason for that." He got up and opened a drawer, extracting a long flat tool of the kind used by professional locksmiths. "This should do the trick."

"Let me guess," Lyn said. "You worked your way through animal training school by stealing cars."

He grinned. "Nope. I just lose keys a lot."

She laughed and followed him outside, discovering another thing she liked about him. She didn't think she'd ever met a man before who would admit to losing anything.

It took Casey approximately three minutes to pop the lock on her car door. Lyn was surprised to feel a twinge of disappointment that the task was so easy, and that there was nothing left for her to do but go home. She turned to him with a smile. "Expertly done," she complimented him. "Thank you. And thank you for dinner."

"Such as it was," he added with a grin. "No problem. I enjoyed your company."

For some reason Lyn found that absurdly flattering. And because it *was* absurd, she added quickly, "I'm sorry I'm such a klutz. I know I've caused you a lot of trouble tonight. I'm usually not like this, honestly—losing cats and getting locked in closets and locking my keys in the car all in one evening. I don't know what's come over me lately. Just a run of bad luck, I guess."

In the light that filtered across the yard from the house, his smile was tender and amused. "I prefer to think of it as destiny. After all, if you hadn't had such a streak of bad luck, we never would have gotten to know each other."

Lyn's pulse stuttered a little with pleasure. "If that's the case," she pointed out, "you manipulated destiny a little when you didn't tell Montana to open the closet."

"So I did." In a playful, unexpected gesture, he reached forward and brushed the tip of her nose with his finger. "Are you sorry?"

She didn't know how to respond to that. She wasn't even sure what the answer was. And, lacking a better alternative, she thrust out her hand with a bright smile and said, "Well, good night and thanks again. It's been a real—adventure, meeting you."

He took her fingers in his, his grip warm and strong. There was a gentle twinkle in his eyes as he responded, "Good night, Lyn Sanders. I'll see you again."

"Yes, of course." She withdrew her hand, not because she wanted to, but because the strength of his touch was doing unexpected things to her equilibrium. "Call us whenever you need us. I think I'm getting the hang of the job now, so you won't have to worry the next time you go away."

He smiled as she retreated toward the car. "I'll call you," he promised.

That sounded very much like the kind of promise a man made to a woman, not a client to a businessperson, but Lyn could have been mistaken. In fact, she decided on the drive home, she was *sure* she was mistaken. Casey Carmichael wasn't interested in her, and even if he was, she wasn't at all sure she approved of the idea. He might be sexy looking and even charming in an offhanded kind of way, but he certainly wasn't her usual type.

As she showered and got ready to watch television in bed at nine o'clock, she reflected on what her usual type was, and it was a depressing composite. Grim, intense, always busy, perpetually dedicated to some higher purpose, not very well groomed and generally distracted . . . That was the kind of man she usually met in her profession, and that was the kind of man she found herself attracted to. And for a good reason, she realized now with an unpleasant start. The men she dated were always more or less a reflection of herself.

Which was another reason a man like Casey Carmichael couldn't possibly be attracted to her, nor she to him. If he did call her, she wouldn't know what to say, and it would only be awkward and embarrassing. Not that it mattered. He would never call.

Casey spent almost half an hour puzzling over the impulsive promise. He wasn't the kind of man who blithely promised a woman he would call her with no intention of doing so, just because he thought that was what she wanted to hear. But he was not going to call Lyn Sanders, and he couldn't understand why he had told her he would.

Casey's relationships with members of the opposite sex were easy and carefree, inevitably self-limiting in nature. He gave little of himself and asked even less in return. Above all, he always made certain there was no possibility anything serious could develop, and at the first sign of anything resembling a genuine involvement he backed quietly and politely away. The women he dated understood that, and expected no more of him than he did of them. Relationships should be purely recreational; they should be *fun*. Anything beyond that was more than he could afford to invest.

Lyn Sanders was a woman who needed to have fun. She had been hurt; he didn't know how or why but he could see barely healed wounds and it was not in his nature to ignore them. She needed a friend. She needed to be challenged, she needed to be busy, she needed to laugh and work and be involved. She needed to start living, for Pete's sake.

And was any of that Casey's responsibility? Of course not. He had learned long ago that he couldn't bring home every stray on the streets, he couldn't mend every broken wing or fill every malnourished belly and if he let himself be consumed by guilt over every needy creature he had to turn away he would have nothing left over for the ones he could save. So he learned to harden his heart, and blind his eyes to the things he couldn't do anything about. It was called being grown-up.

Of course, sometimes he still slipped....

But not with Lyn Sanders. She was not a stray puppy or a wounded kitten and she needed more than a little first aid and a sense of security. He was very much afraid that she needed more than he could afford to give.

Thus resolved, he made his routine night check of the kennel and the livestock, and turned the cats out into the living room to play. He hated to leave them penned up all day; it wasn't good for his regimen or theirs. He would have to double up on the dogs' exercise tomorrow, and the horses were overdue for a good, hard run. He hoped that his kennel boy recovered from whatever he had and got back to work quickly. This was really a two-man operation.

He tossed balls and dangled strings for the cats, chuckling at their antics, and when they had worn down some of their nervous energy he started putting a few of them through their routines. But he couldn't concentrate. He kept seeing the shadows of pain in Lyn Sanders's eyes, the vulnerable curve of her mouth. He kept hearing her laugh, and remembering what a nice contrast that was to the uncertainty he saw in her smile at other times.

He liked it when her temper flared. He liked the way she looked him in the eyes and told him what she thought. He didn't like it when she backed away. He didn't like to think of her spending her days all alone in her sister's house, trying to think of new and improved ways to do nothing.

Not that it was any of his business. Not that he cared.

On the other hand, she was only going to be here for a short while. What would it hurt to invite her to spend some of that time with him? They could have fun together, get to know each other better.

After a moment he got up and idly flipped through his Rolodex until he found the Pet Pride card. He looked at it for a moment, then closed the Rolodex.

Not that it mattered. He wasn't going to call.

The phone began to ring at a quarter to eight. Lyn groaned and pulled the pillow over her head. She had an hour before she had to get up to feed the Greshams' cats, and she couldn't think of a single person she wanted to talk to at this hour of the day.

The ringing went on and on, and she burrowed deeper under the pillow, determined to ignore it. Except that it could be Pat. Or, heaven forbid, a client. She cursed herself for not putting the answering machine on last night and at last reached over and fumbled for the phone on the nightstand. She dropped the receiver on the floor with a thud, and had to pull it over the side of the bed by the cord. She hoped that by that time the party on the other end would have hung up, but no such luck. An unforgivably cheerful male voice responded to her muffled, "Hello."

"Good morning. This is Casey Carmichael. How would you like to go on a picnic today?"

The moment he spoke his name her heart started speeding wakefulness through her veins and she struggled to a half-sitting position, pushing her hair out of her eyes. "Casey? What? What are you doing calling this time of day?"

"I just invited you on a picnic. You weren't still asleep were you?"

"No," she lied. She sat up straighter, smoothing down the covers and straightening the shoulders of her nightgown. "No, of course not. It's just that I wasn't expecting to hear from you."

Then she was annoyed with herself. *Lots* of people were still asleep at seven forty-five in the morning. No one with any manners called before eight, anyway; what was she feeling defensive about?

"I told you I'd call," he reminded her. "So how about it?"

Picnic, her fuzzy brain reminded her. He'd just invited her on a picnic, and before she'd even had her breakfast. She was quite certain she couldn't deal with this. She wasn't even sure she wanted to go out with him at all, and she simply wasn't capable of making that kind of decision before she'd had her coffee.

She said, "Um...no, I can't. I have cats and fish to feed."

"What time?"

"Well...two times. Nine and five. But that's not the point—"

"No problem. I'll pick you up at eleven and we'll be back in plenty of time for the second shift."

"But—"

"And listen, do you mind packing lunch? I don't have anything in the house but peanut butter."

"What? But you—"

"Thanks. I'll bring the wine. I'll see you at eleven."

"—invited *me!*" Lyn sputtered into a dead phone. He had hung up.

She spent almost a full minute staring at the receiver in her hand, and by the time she replaced it none too gently in its cradle she was fuming. Whoever heard of inviting a woman on a picnic and then telling *her* to bring lunch? She hadn't even told him she would go. She didn't even *want* to go. And wouldn't he be surprised when he got here at eleven o'clock and found out she wasn't even home?

She wasn't accustomed to being this upset this early in the morning, and the rise in blood pressure gave her a slight headache. She couldn't go back to sleep now, and that was another thing she had to thank Casey Carmichael for. She hadn't been up before eight-thirty of her own free will since she'd come here.

She took a cup of coffee to the pool patio and alternately seethed and brooded until it was time to leave to feed the cats. Who did he think he was, anyway? Obviously, he was a man used to giving orders—but to dogs, not people. He had a thing or two to learn about human relations, that was certain. Unfortunately Lyn had neither the energy nor the inclination to be the one to teach him.

But when the cats were fed and the beagle was walked, Lyn found herself standing in front of the open refrigerator wondering if Pat had anything on hand suitable for making a picnic lunch. It wasn't that she was the type of woman who enjoyed being bossed around by presumptuous, overbearing men; she was merely anticipating how delightful it would be to watch Casey Carmichael's face as he bit into a sandwich composed entirely of jalapeño peppers.

The day had brightened into the relentless perfection Lyn had come to expect of Florida. The sky was flat and blue, decorated with a few wispy clouds high in the atmosphere. The breeze was balmy. The temperature was in the high seventies. It was a perfect day for a picnic and she had known since the moment she had picked up the phone and heard his voice that she was going to go. Casey Carmichael not only made it impossible to say no; he made it impossible to *want* to say no. And a man like that, irritating as he could be, was worth getting to know a little better.

Without debating the matter another minute, Lyn hurried to her room to change her clothes. After all, he had hardly seen her at her best last night, and when he arrived this morning he would be in for more than one surprise.

Four

Casey pulled into her driveway in a mud-splattered Jeep at ten minutes before eleven. Lyn met him on the front steps, picnic basket in hand. When he reached her, she thrust the basket into his hands.

"Peanut butter," she said, unsmiling. "That's all I had in the house."

A slow abashed grin spread over his face as he looked from her to the basket. "I guess it was a little thoughtless of me to ask you to fix lunch, wasn't it?"

"It certainly was," Lyn agreed, although he did score points for admitting his mistake as soon as it was pointed out to him.

"I guess I could have offered to pick something up on the way."

"There's a thought."

The little-boy grin would have annoyed her if it were worn by someone else, but on him it looked perfectly

sincere, utterly natural. "Sorry," he said. "I guess social skills aren't high on my list of priorities. I should
practice more. I did bring the wine, though, and peanut
butter happens to be one of my favorite foods."

She allowed him to coax a grudging smile from her.
"Well," she admitted, "I did throw in a few apples and
some cheese, so we won't starve. Where are we going?"

"Rainbow Lake." He placed a light, companionable
hand on her shoulder as he gestured her down the steps.
"It's not far from here, and there's a nice little park
around it. Not many people go there," he added practically, "so it's a good place to exercise the dogs."

As they reached the Jeep, Lyn saw the two collies securely seatbelted in the back seat, and she couldn't help
wondering if she were an afterthought to the dogs' play-
time. But the slight prickle of disappointment she felt was
immediately wiped away as he helped her into the Jeep.

"You look pretty," he said.

She was wearing a violet tank top and lavender print
boxer shorts, with a loose-fitting white cotton shirt to
protect her shoulders from the sun. She had drawn her
hair up into a curly ponytail topped with a sun visor, and
had even added a touch of blush to her normally color-
less cheeks. His eyes traced the way the tank top hugged
her breasts and her waist, and lingered on the line of her
legs as she swung them into the vehicle, and Lyn felt a
tingle of gratification. How long had it been since a man
looked at her like that? Then again, how often had she
had a chance to wear shorts or go on picnics in Philadelphia? She was glad she had accepted his invitation . . . even if she had been an afterthought.

Her eyes twinkled as she replied, "Thank you. You
look different too—with your clothes on."

He laughed and went around to the other side of the Jeep storing the picnic basket in the back on his way. He was dressed very respectably today in jeans, sneakers, and a polo shirt; the soft fabric of the jeans hugged his thighs and the pale peach color of the shirt made his skin look golden. He seemed to grow more attractive every time Lyn saw him.

He grasped the steering wheel and pulled himself onto the driver's seat, his eyes still glinting as he commented, "You know what they say. If you want to get to know a person, take off his clothes and lock him in a closet."

Lyn choked back a bubble of laughter. "Is that what they say?"

"Sure. A naked man has a tendency to be very sincere."

"Ha! I know a lot of loved-and-left women who'd disagree with that."

He darted a glance at her as he backed out of the driveway. "Not you, I hope."

She shrugged uncomfortably and adjusted her visor to shade her eyes. "I never had time to be loved or left. Besides, I think this conversation is getting too personal."

"I didn't think we had any secrets."

"I think you take a lot for granted."

"Another one of my faults," he replied, changing gears. "It's a waste of time to leave these things to chance. Fasten your seat belt."

Lyn glanced at him, wondering if she would ever figure him out. One moment he was brash and overbearing, the next charming and likable. One moment he made her laugh, the next she wondered why she had ever agreed to this outing. He was definitely a challenge, and the last thing she needed at this point in her life was a challenge.

But, she decided as she fastened her seat belt, she was in it this far. She might as well enjoy the ride.

The wind whipping through the open Jeep made conversation difficult, which was probably for the best. Casey Carmichael was much more enjoyable company when he was not talking. The wind buffeted his gold-streaked hair and the sun narrowed his eyes and glinted with specks of bronze on the backs of his arms. His fingers tapped out a rhythm to an unheard tune on the steering wheel, and every now and then he would glance at Lyn and smile. Lyn smiled back, because that was another thing about Casey Carmichael: his good humor was impossible to resist.

There were so many lakes and recreation areas in central Florida that after a while they all started to look alike; Lyn could not say for sure whether she had ever been to Rainbow Lake before. She did know that it was one of the prettiest spots she had seen. Devoid of the usual proliferation of campers and mobile homes, a wide green park dotted with cypress and lavishly planted with beds of colorful flowers surrounded a mirror-flat lake, and only three of the dozens of outdoor tables were occupied. When Casey released the dogs they had almost an acre of open grass in which to run before they reached the picnic area.

Removing the picnic basket from the back of the Jeep, Casey said, "Let's go down to the lake. I've got a blanket, and there's a gazebo down there that we can take shelter in if the sun gets too hot."

"Sounds fine."

He handed her the basket, and reached back inside for two butterfly nets and a small screened cage. Lyn stared at the new equipment.

"What's that?"

"I have to have a couple of dozen butterflies for a shoot tomorrow," he explained. "This is a good place for them, so I thought we could gather them up after lunch."

Lyn said carefully, "You asked me out here to catch butterflies with you?"

"No," he replied reasonably. "I asked you out here because I like you, and wanted to get to know you better. But I didn't see any reason why we couldn't get a little work done in the meantime."

Lyn released a long slow breath. "You," she said, "are the most controlling, manipulative person I have ever met." And then, surprising herself, she added, "I think I admire that in a man."

He grinned and draped his arm around her shoulders as they moved toward the lake. "That's good. Because I think it's too late for me to change now."

"I didn't say there wasn't room for improvement," she pointed out, but her tone was not as severe as it could have been.

It was hard to be stern about anything with the sun dancing in her eyes and the warm circle of his arm tingling through her shoulders, flushing her skin. He had an easy, natural touch, unlike the awkwardness of some men, which made intimacy seem forced. Perhaps it was his confidence that made being near him a soothing experience; the same single-minded certainty that Lyn sometimes found so irritating was also the thing that made his presence so comfortable. She always knew where she stood with him.

He spread the blanket in the sun a few feet from the lake and they settled down with the picnic basket between them, gazing out over the water. The collies ran and jumped along the shoreline, occasionally venturing

into the water but always staying in sight of their master.
Lyn smiled as she watched them play.

"How did you get into animal training?" she asked.

Casey glanced at her. He was lounging back on one elbow, the material of his shirt pulled taut across his chest.
Sunlight played in his eyes and highlighted the planes of
his face as he smiled. "That's a long, boring story. I'd
rather talk about you."

"I doubt that," Lyn replied. "I've never met a man yet
who didn't prefer talking about himself to anything else
under the sun."

He chuckled. "Funny. I was just going to say the same
thing about the women I've known. Maybe it depends on
who you're with. I can tell you about me anytime, but
you're a mystery. And I'm interested."

Lyn lifted her shoulders in what she hoped was a light
gesture. "There's nothing mysterious about me. I've led
a dull, ordinary life. You're the one with a cougar in your
bathroom."

Casey plucked a long stem of grass and lifted it to her
face, drawing the feathery tip of it down the curve of her
cheek until she looked at him. The gesture was playful,
but the sensation was not. His eyes were as rich as the
colors of springtime, as deep and promising. Lyn felt her
throat tighten, just with looking at him, and the gentle
stroking caress of the blade of grass against her cheek
caused a prickling sensation in her breasts.

She turned her face away from his touch, and after a
moment he tossed the blade of grass away.

"Actually," he said in a conversational tone, "it's not
such a boring story at that. My folks died when I was a
kid, and I was raised by my grandmother. She was a good
soul, but a little old for a rambunctious teenager. The
only thing she ever asked of me was that I finish high

school, and she made damn sure I did that. The day after graduation, though, I was out of there. I ran away and joined the circus."

And a week after that, his grandmother had died. The news hadn't reached him until almost a month later. And because he was still just a kid, he had not realized how much he loved her, how much he needed her, until she was gone. He had never forgiven himself for that. He had never forgiven himself for not being with her when she died, and had never stopped wondering whether it was his actions that had brought on her final heart attack.

Casey's face was in shadow, and Lyn did not see the flicker of sober memory that crossed his eyes. He made certain she didn't hear anything in his voice.

She gave a startled laugh. "Are you serious? You're making that up! People don't really run away to join the circus."

Casey relaxed, smoothing out his features. "This one did. I signed on as an apprentice to the animal handler, which sounded like a real glamour job. What it meant was mucking out stalls and cleaning up after the elephants twelve hours a day. If I worked fast, though, I could usually get a chance to watch the handler go through his routine, and I guess I learned a few things— that I didn't want to clean up after elephants for the rest of my life, for one. I left the circus after a year and worked my way through college showing dogs—and if you think *that* wasn't a hassle, trying to work in classes around the dog show circuit. Fortunately," he added modestly, "I was pretty smart, so I got a couple of scholarships, too. I ended up with a degree in behavioral psychology and a breeding pair of cocker spaniels, and the rest, as they say, is history."

Lyn laughed softly. "You call that a dull story?"

He grinned. "I left out the sexy parts."

"I guess you did. What does a psychology degree have to do with doing cat food commercials?"

"More than you'd guess. It allows me to be my own boss, for one thing, and do something I like. And because animals are generally less neurotic than people, I can keep a pretty healthy psyche myself."

"Because you're always in control."

Their eyes met, and held. His gaze was steady and unashamed, not a warning, merely an honest statement of fact as he answered, "Right."

Lyn looked away, knowing before he spoke what he was going to say. "Now your turn. Tell me about yourself."

"Like what?"

"Like why you left Philadelphia, what you like for breakfast, whether or not you're married..."

She laughed, answering only the last question. "Not married. Never even came close." But it seemed like a fair question so she glanced at him. "What about you?"

He shook his head. And then for some reason he felt compelled to add, "I was engaged once. We shared a little apartment off-campus for over a year. She was killed in a car accident three weeks before the wedding."

Casey had not blamed her, or the drunk driver who proceeded down a dark one-way street without his headlights on. He had blamed himself...for not being behind the wheel, for the minor argument they had had that sent her out into the night alone. For caring too much, for loving too intensely. Because it had become clear that the pattern of love was loss, and he had learned to control what he could and let the rest pass him by. It was not an easy way to live, but it was the only way he knew how.

Lyn murmured, "I'm sorry." And the silence that followed was pained and uncomfortable. What was it about her that compelled him to tell the absolute truth, sharing too much, revealing more than she had a right to know, opening himself far too easily? He had to be careful around her, he realized. She was more dangerous than she knew.

He turned the focus back to Lyn, where it should have been in the first place. "Why did you leave your job in Philadelphia?"

She drew up her knees and encircled them with her arms, directing her attention to the lake. He had told her things in the past few minutes that could not have been easy for him, and it only seemed fair that she reciprocate the intimacy. But maybe he was stronger than she was, more accustomed to dealing with painful memories. She wasn't ready to be that open yet.

She answered, as truthfully as she could, "I don't know. I grew up I guess. I got into social work thinking I could change the world, but I found out nothing anybody can do makes a difference. Too many bad guys, too few good guys. I got tired of wasting my time."

Casey knew that feeling. All too well. "So you just gave up."

She tensed. "I got smart."

His easy tone surprised her as he replied, "Nothing wrong with that, I suppose. So are you going to stay in Florida now?"

She looked at him, grateful once again for his refusal to pry, and then she remembered he was a psychologist. He knew when to push and when to back away, and his timing was impeccable. She would definitely have to watch her step around him from now on.

She smiled in secret amusement at how easily he had almost manipulated her again, and answered, "I'm not sure yet. It's tempting, though. There's something about this place—all the sunshine and humidity I guess—that makes you feel like you're on vacation all the time. Like it's just too much effort to worry about anything, or do anything important. I like that."

"The Tahiti syndrome," Casey replied negligently. "It'll wear off after you've been here a while."

"I hope not."

"Did anyone ever tell you you have fantastic legs?"

A startled little surge of heat sprang from the tips of her toes and flowed upward to tickle the back of her throat. When she looked at him his eyes were roaming with unabashed appreciation from the curve of her up-drawn thighs to her ankles, and delight sparkled in her eyes as she watched him.

"Did anyone ever tell you," she responded, "that you're outrageous?"

"Constantly." He grinned and caught her hand, pulling her to her feet. "Let's go catch some butterflies."

For the next hour they crept through the jungle of bougainvillea and hibiscus, stalking their prey. The first time Lyn snared a butterfly she squealed so loudly with excitement that she frightened the dogs into frantic barking and no further specimens were to be found on that side of the lake. The sun beat down, frizzing Lyn's hair and dampening the back of her shirt; it was tedious and sometimes frustrating work, but Lyn could not remember having had so much fun since she was a child. In many ways, being with Casey *was* like being a child again; he made laughter easy and worry hard, and nothing seemed very important except the moment.

When they stopped for lunch six butterflies were resting on the clump of grass in the bottom of the cage, which Casey considered an extraordinary catch.

"What are you going to do with them?" she asked, pushing her heavy ponytail off her neck as she sank to the blanket.

"I'm not really sure." Casey opened the bottle of white wine and poured two paper cups full. "Some kind of soap commercial. They just call me up and tell me what they need and I get it for them if I can."

"But butterflies. Seems like an odd request to make of an animal trainer."

"That's nothing." He handed her a cup of wine. "You should have been here the time I had to get a hundred spiders on the set for a horror movie. Or the bees. Now *that* was an experience to remember."

"I guess I should count myself lucky I didn't know you back then, or you'd have me out here with a beekeeper's hat and gloves, shaking honey trees."

He smiled. "I don't know. I think it would have been nice to know you back then."

"So I could help you catch bees?"

"No." His eyes were sun drowsy and backlit with warmth as he lifted his cup to her in a small toast. "Just to know you."

Lyn felt a catch in her throat at the unexpected sweetness of the sentiment, and she quickly lowered her eyes to her cup as she took a sip of wine. Just when she thought she had him figured out, he had to do something endearing, catching her off guard and making her uncertain again. Clearly, Casey Carmichael was a complication in her life she couldn't afford...and yet she wasn't entirely sure he was an unwelcome one, either.

They feasted on cheese and apples, and Casey scolded Lyn playfully for feeding her peanut butter sandwich to the dogs, piece by piece.

"They're twins." Lyn lazily observed the dogs, leaning back on one elbow to sip her wine. "A lot of your animals are."

"I try to work them in pairs. That way, I can double the number of tricks they can do, and if one doesn't feel like performing on a particular day we don't have to shut down the set."

"Makes sense. Except for Grizabella. There's only one of her."

He made an expression of distaste. "Which makes one too many. That's what happens when you let advertising people take over—they gave me the cat and told me to make her a star, thinking that just because she could trace her ancestry back to Queen Victoria she had to be a genius. Dumbest damn cat I ever saw."

Lyn chuckled, rolling over to her side to look at him. "She's sold a lot of cat food."

"Maybe. But give me a good honest mutt who wouldn't recognize his mother on the street any day."

His eyes followed the curve of her jaw and the slope of her neck with absent pleasure, resting at last on the dip of her cleavage where the position of her arm pushed her breasts together. She had taken off her outer shirt as the day grew hotter, and the skinny tank top molded the long line of her torso, clinging to her skin where a line of perspiration dampened the material between her breasts. Casey felt the pace of his pulse increase as he followed that dark line down her sternum until it disappeared inside her shorts, and he could not help imagining his fingers tracing the path along soft, slippery skin. He wondered if she had any idea how sexy she was. He wondered if she would object if he told her . . . or showed her.

She said, "Where do you get all your animals?"

He raised his eyes to her face again, and drew his thoughts away from their errant course. "From the pound mostly." He took a sip of wine to hide a slight expression of bitterness as he added, "You'd be surprised what Americans throw out with the garbage."

"So," Lyn said softly, "you do care."

He was surprised. "What?"

"You said your animals were just a job, and you never got attached to them. But I think you're just an old softie at heart."

That made him uncomfortable. Casey was not used to people analyzing him, seeing through him, drawing conclusions that were better left unspoken—even if they were the correct ones. Had the observation come from another woman he would have closed her out solidly, or deftly turned her away with a joke. But because it was Lyn, because the quiet, open way she looked at him suggested a kind of intimacy he had never expected from her, he was taken off guard. He didn't feel threatened, he felt—touched. Pleased. And he couldn't push her away, not entirely.

The smile that curved his lips was wistful; his eyes shadowed as he looked down into his wine. "Honey—" the endearment came out so naturally that she barely noticed it "—I haven't been attached to anyone or anything since I was a kid. I don't think I'm capable of it anymore." He looked at her, and his eyes held a quiet honesty with no regret. "You should remember that."

Lyn looked across the blanket to where one of the collies was lying with its head between its paws, eagerly watching their every move in case a scrap of food should happen to be tossed his way. She wanted to ask him why, to know what had happened to make him so guarded...and then she didn't want to know. She didn't want the responsibility of hearing what he might tell her, she didn't want to risk understanding, and perhaps caring. She wanted to keep it simple.

"I know what you mean," she said lightly, though her heart was beating a little faster than normal. "In my line of work, you learn early not to get too involved. It gets to be a habit after a while."

He smiled. "I don't think you're the kind of person who could ever stay uninvolved. In fact, if I had to guess, I'd say your problem is that you care too much."

Before she could ask what he meant by that, he sat up to refill his cup and changed the subject. "Are you having a good time?"

"Hmm." She cradled her head on her folded arm and nodded drowsily. "I really am."

"Me, too. It's not often I get a chance to do nothing."

Lyn laughed, spilling some of the wine that he had recently poured into her cup. "Chasing butterflies around a three-acre lake is your idea of doing nothing? I don't think I've had so much exercise since I came to Florida."

"A little honest butterfly chasing never hurt anybody." His eyes crinkled as he stretched out beside her, his weight resting on his elbows, his ankles crossed and his head tilted back. His clean masculine scent was as warm as sunshine, and he was so close that the fine, gold-tinted hairs along the back of his arm brushed against her bare shoulder. She could hear his soft breathing, the day was so still, and for a time she was fascinated by the rhythmic rise and fall of his breast muscles against the material of his shirt.

She looked at his face and found him gazing down at her with the same sort of lazy absorption with which she had been observing him. The hint of a smile was in his eyes, and cloud shadows drifted slowly overhead, lightening and darkening the smooth planes of his face. She felt her skin tighten in anticipation as he shifted slightly, lifting his hand to brush away the curl that clung to her cheek.

He said, "I've never known a redhead with gray eyes before."

His fingertips lingered on her face, lightly stroking the curve of her earlobe. Lyn's breath was thin and her throat felt husky as she replied, "I think it's going to rain."

Radiating lines appeared around his eyes with his smile. "That's a non sequitur if I ever heard one."

She knew she should do something to break the spell, but she didn't quite have the will. The sun and the wine made her lethargic, and the gentle caress of his fingers on her skin worked its own energy-stripping magic. So she merely pointed out, without much conviction, "We still have butterflies to catch."

"They're not going anywhere."

His fingers drifted over her jawline, and lingered for a moment on her throat. Lyn's pulse speeded with the touch. She lifted her eyes to his. "Casey," she asked softly, "why did you ask me here today?"

He could have answered in a dozen different ways, and all of them would have been the truth. He could have ignored the question, and gently turned her delicate, slightly parted lips to his, which at that moment was above all things in the world what he wanted to do. But caution reasserted itself, and common sense. Sometimes he was led far too much by his instincts, and where Lyn was concerned he wasn't at all sure his instincts could be trusted.

So, after a moment's hesitation, he lifted his hand to her hair, playfully adjusted her visor, and whatever tenuous magic that had begun between them was gone. He said, "Aside from the fact that I like you and thought you needed something more interesting to do than lie around the house sleeping till five o'clock in the afternoon? I'm glad you asked."

He sat up, and Lyn, feeling far too vulnerable to remain lying down, reluctantly did the same. He finished the last of his wine and said, "As a matter of fact, I have a proposition for you. It turns out that my kennel boy doesn't have the flu, he has mono. Now I know you don't hear much about that nowadays, but that's the way it is, and he won't be back to work for a month at least. So how would you like a job?"

That was the last thing she had expected to hear him say, and for a moment shock—and disappointment— were so bitter in her throat that she couldn't even speak. At last she managed, "Kennel boy? You want me to be your *kennel boy*?"

He held up a hand as though to forestall the outrage that must have been forming in her eyes. "No, let me rephrase that. I wouldn't ask you to do kennel work—I can take care of that part until I can hire some high-school kid. But Joey really left me in a bind. He had just gotten to the point where he was a big help in training, and the behaviors go a lot faster with an assistant. It's not hard work, but it sure would be a help to me."

When he put it like that, Lyn's rancor seemed misplaced. She still did not find the proposal in the least bit appealing, but it didn't sound like quite the insult it had been at the beginning. She said, "I don't think so. I mean, I've still got Pat's business to run—"

"It would only be a couple or three hours a day," he said, "and no real physical labor. You might even enjoy it."

She was already shaking her head. "No, you don't understand. These last two pet-sitting jobs are over tomorrow and we don't have anything else lined up—"

"Perfect."

"*And*," she continued firmly, "I was looking forward to having some time off while Pat's away, to just relax and have a vacation."

Casey said perceptively, "From what you've told me, it sounds as though you've been on vacation since you got here."

She bristled unaccountably. "So? There's nothing wrong with that. That's what people come to Florida for!"

"Everyone needs a job, Lyn," Casey said gently. "Even burned-out social workers with no direction in life."

She scowled sharply. "So is that what this is—some kind of therapy?"

His smile was so easy that it was impossible to suspect the motives behind it. "Maybe it's just a way to guarantee that I get to see more of you."

Lyn dropped her eyes uncomfortably. "Well…thanks but no thanks. I'm not very good with animals, you've seen that for yourself. And I don't want a job."

"I wouldn't be so hasty if I were you. The pay isn't much, but the fringe benefits are out of this world."

She glanced at him, then quickly away, afraid to ask what those fringe benefits might be. She said, "I'm not interested. I don't want to get involved in anything, or be responsible for anything right now. I like things the way they are.''

''I think a little responsibility is just what you need right now to take your mind off your troubles.''

''I told you, I'm not interested.''

He was unfazed. ''You think about it,'' he advised. And, without giving her a chance for further argument he caught her hand. ''Now, let's see about those butterflies. We need to get at least a dozen more before we can start home.''

They had not spotted the first butterfly when the rain came. It blew up suddenly, the way rain showers in Florida often did, with an abrupt graying of the sky, a gust of wind, and a downpour. The dogs, who were a good deal smarter than their human companions, raced for the car while Lyn and Casey struggled with the unwieldly butterfly nets and the wire cage.

''The blanket!'' Lyn cried, gesturing back toward the picnic area. ''It's going to get soaked!''

''Too late!'' Casey grabbed her hand and they raced toward the shelter of the small gazebo at the edge of the lake.

The grass was slippery and Lyn almost lost her footing more than once, each time only Casey's strong arm saved her. By the time they reached the shelter, gasping and laughing, the violence of the downpour had lightened to a steady drumming on the gazebo roof, but they were both drenched through. Lyn's hair was a heavy mass at the back of her neck, dripping rivulets of water over her shoulders and her face, the polished cotton shorts clung limply to her legs, and the tank top was molded to her body, clearly showing the shape of her nipples, which were puckered with the cold. Casey pushed his hand over his face, wiping the water out of his eyes, then shook his head, spraying water everywhere and laughing as Lyn squealed and stepped back.

"The poor butterflies!" she exclaimed, examining the wire cage. "They're all wet!"

"They'll survive," Casey assured her and took the cage from her.

"But we still need more." Lyn wrung out the hem of her shorts. "We'll never get another dozen now."

"Trick photography," Casey assured her. "It can make half a dozen butterflies look like a hundred."

That was when she noticed an odd, almost absent tone to his voice, and when she looked up he was standing very close, looking down at her and smiling. "What?" she said nervously, pushing at the wet tendrils of hair that shadowed her forehead. "Do I look like a drowned rat?"

The smile deepened, and he took a step forward, so that his thighs were almost brushing hers. Lightly he dropped his hands onto her shoulders. "You look," he told her, "like a mermaid."

"Is that supposed to be a compliment?" Her voice was a little breathless as she looked up at him. His touch, the gentle murmur of the rain, the soft light in his eyes seemed to draw a blanket of intimacy and expectation around them. Despite the chill rain, Lyn felt flushed. She didn't seem to be able to take her eyes from his.

"It's a compliment," Casey told her. His finger came up and wiped a trickle of rain from her throat. "Your face looks like it's covered with dew, and your eyes are the color of morning."

He lowered his face and she felt the gentle brush of the tip of his tongue against her cheek, tasting the rain. Lyn did not breathe. A melting sensation of paralysis went through her muscles with the warm flood of his breath across her face, the whisper-soft touch of his tongue

against her temple, the lobe of her ear, the tip of her nose.
Somehow her hands were resting on his waist, and she
could feel the heat of his flesh beneath the wet material,
the tensing and lengthening of lean muscles as he leaned
forward, teasing the droplets of rain from her skin.

With each brush of his lips or tongue across her face a
new set of nerve endings flared to life, a new flutter of
heat leaped into her veins. The rush and roar of her
heartbeat was in counterrhythm to the steady pulse of
rain on the gazebo roof, and her breath was a thin shallow stream through parted lips. When his mouth brushed
hers she instinctively turned into the caress, drawing him
close, sinking into his embrace.

Casey let the last of his self-restraint slip away as he
drew her mouth to his, tasting her, holding her, and the
truth was he didn't have a choice. He could no longer remember why it had seemed so important to back away
before, and keeping his distance from her seemed like the
most absurd intention he had ever had. He couldn't resist her. He didn't want to. And it was more than just this
moment, the warmth of her rain-bathed skin melding
with his, her wildflower scent enveloping him, the simple *feel* of her, inside his head, inside his skin. His pulses
soared and fever flared and he couldn't think what was
best anymore. He didn't want to think. He wanted this
kiss to go on forever. He wanted to lower her to the
ground and slip her clothes aside and explore every curve
and hidden recess of her body; he wanted to bury himself with her, to drown inside her. He wanted to hold her,
to be a part of her, to let himself be absorbed in her and
her in him, and he wanted it to last for a very long time.
And he couldn't think of a single reason any of that
should not come to pass. He could not remember why
once he had warned himself not to get too close to her.

Lyn tasted the smooth heat of his tongue in an explosion of dizziness and color, a flood of intense awareness that invaded her senses and left her weak. Dimly she was aware of his fingers, strong and hard, on her back, and the texture of his damp jeans against her bare thighs. A smothered moan escaped her and her arms, with a will of their own, encircled him, fingertips pressing into his neck, holding him close. He tasted of wine and rain. He filled her with heat and a swirling pattern of light and dark. Her heart was thundering, and she couldn't separate her own breath from his.

His mouth left hers, brushing across the line of her jaw, pressing long and deep into her throat. His hands slid up her rib cage until they cupped her heavy, aching breasts and everything within Lyn seemed to stop, wanting and not wanting, suspended in anticipation of his touch. Only the thin layer of material separated her flesh from the heat of his touch, and when his fingertips began to stroke her breasts, tracing their shape and fullness with an electric touch, it was as though nothing separated them at all. Darts of pleasure tightened in her loins as he encircled her swollen nipples, surges of helpless, aching need. She wanted to sink into it, she wanted to surrender to the powerful, demanding world of sensation he created, and in another moment that was exactly what she would have done.

She closed her fingers around his wrists; she whispered, "Casey...don't. Stop. Please."

His hands slid down to her waist; he pressed a long kiss against the curve of her collarbone. His breath was an uneven flood against her skin and she could feel his heartbeat thundering against hers as he whispered, "Come home with me."

"No," she replied hoarsely, and with a great effort. She forced herself to open her eyes, to take his arms again and take a small step backward. Her breath came in erratic leaps and starts, her muscles ached, and even her skin felt raw, abraded by his touch. "No," she repeated, with slightly more conviction.

His eyes were soft-bright, deep and penetrating. "Why?"

The remnants of passion still flushed his skin, and dark blond curls clung damply to his forehead. It was all Lyn could do to keep her hand from lifting, and smoothing back those curls. She tightened her hands into fists; she forced steadiness into her voice. She said, "Because—this is ridiculous. It's too fast. I—I don't even know you."

And then Casey remembered why. He remembered the danger of moving too fast, of wanting too much. How easy it was to forget with Lyn, how hard it was to turn away. But when he smiled, and lifted his hand to stroke her cheek, that was exactly what he intended to do. Turn away.

He heard himself saying instead, "I know how to fix that. Come work for me."

"I—no." She forced herself to turn away from his caress, taking a deep breath. "I told you, I don't want to get involved." She looked at him, making her tone as firm as she could. "I don't think this is a good idea, Casey."

His smile was too gentle, too patient. "Think about it."

"No." She took another breath. "The rain has stopped. We should start back."

She reached for the butterfly cage at the same time he did. Their hands brushed, and she automatically jerked back. His smile deepened. "Think about it," he repeated.

"No."

But she knew even before she looked into his tolerant, amused eyes, that she would think about it, and think about it a great deal. And she knew, as much as she tried to deny it, what her answer would eventually be.

Casey knew it, too, and he was not at all certain whether he was glad, or sorry.

Five

For the next three days, Lyn did nothing but think about Casey Carmichael. He called, but only to ask her to feed the animals while he did the television commercial. She managed without incident, and did not see him. He didn't ask whether or not she had reconsidered his job offer, and she certainly was not about to bring the subject up. Casey Carmichael was a dangerous man, and the less she saw of him, the better.

She went to bed early, she slept late, she watched day-time game shows and flipped through magazines. She talked to Pat twice long-distance and told her everything was going fine. With no new pet-sitting jobs on the horizon she had hours and hours of nothing to do, which was exactly what she wanted. And she filled most of those hours thinking about Casey.

She knew what he was doing, of course. He didn't want to be accused of forcing her into anything, so he was biding his time. She would come to him on his terms, or not at all. And Lyn had no intention of playing that game. She wasn't interested in Casey Carmichael, or his job. She liked her life the way it was.

But when the phone rang with an offer of a pet-sitting job not too far from Pat's house, Lyn leaped at the opportunity with uncharacteristic enthusiasm. Anything to take her mind off smiling emerald eyes and strong caressing hands.

The woman who had called identified herself as Jane Crebs, and said that she bred Himalayan cats. She had a chance to go to California for two weeks and needed someone to check in on her cats once every other day while she was gone. Although Pat had no objection to taking on new clients, especially during the slow season, she had warned Lyn to make certain she did not commit to any new jobs over the phone. So Lyn made an appointment to see Mrs. Crebs and her cats that afternoon.

The Crebs house was in an older neighborhood, across the street from a small lake and shaded by big live oaks that were rare in the citrus section of Florida. The first thing Lyn noticed as she pulled into the driveway was a black-and-white dog tied to a tree, and she was mildly dismayed. The woman had not said anything about a dog.

When she got out of her car, her dismay grew. The dog did not get up, or bark, and as Lyn walked closer she saw why—the chain to which it was attached was so short Lyn doubted the animal *could* stand up. It lay with its ears flattened and its tail tightly hugging its body, watching Lyn with wary, suspicious eyes. Lyn did not know enough about dogs to realize that such behavior could often indicate a biter, so she walked over to it, speaking softly.

Fortunately the dog was either too weak, dispirited or tied too tightly to bite. It made a low sound in its throat that could have been a whine or a growl, thumped its tail once, and closed its eyes as though in submission to whatever Lyn cared to do to it.

The dog's coat was filthy and matted, its eyes were runny, and she could see the shape of his ribs beneath the fur. There wasn't a water dish anywhere in sight. "You poor thing," Lyn murmured, and bent down to stroke the dog's head.

Just then the front door opened, and a voice called out, "I wouldn't touch that animal if I was you. No telling what kind of diseases he's got."

Lyn straightened up and started up the steps. "Mrs. Crebs? I'm Lyn Sanders with Pet Pride."

Mrs. Crebs was a large woman in a too-short muumuu who returned Lyn's handshake with a single perfunctory pump. "Good to meet you. Come on in."

"You didn't mention you had a dog."

Mrs. Crebs cast a disinterested glance over her shoulder. "What, that mangy old thing? It's not mine. Some old stray that been digging up gardens and turning over trash cans. My husband wanted to shoot it, but I caught it this morning and tied it up. Just waiting for the pound to come pick it up now."

Lyn started to timidly point out that the dog had no water and its chain was too short, but just then more pressing concerns took her attention.

The moment she walked into the house the odor was overwhelming. As Mrs. Crebs led the way to the back room the reason immediately became apparent. The woman didn't just have cats; she had *cats*, dozens of them. They were stacked like canned goods against the walls in cages no bigger than airline carriers, from the floor upward, one on top of the other. Some of them yowled, some of them hissed and spit as Lyn walked by, some of them were sleeping in their litter and didn't seem to be able to manage more than a dull, disinterested glance before closing their eyes again.

Lyn's stomach turned as she looked around. Water dishes were clouded with bits of food or empty altogether, coats were tangled, kittens were crowded four and five to a cage. She managed, in a somewhat strangled voice, "You—*breed* these cats? For a living?"

Mrs. Crebs gave a short nod. "Easiest thing in the world. Cats don't need much looking after, you see. Fill up their food and water dishes once in a while and when they're empty, fill them again. That's why I think you'll only need to come by once every other day. Ten dollars a visit, did you say it was?"

Lyn barely heard her. Her eyes were moving in slow disgust from cage to cage. When she thought about Casey's luxury condos for his cats, the expensive diet formulas, the spotless living quarters, this charnel house seemed even worse than it was. She felt slow outrage boiling inside her. "And people—pay you for these kittens?"

Now Mrs. Crebs began to look a little insulted. "Well, of course I have to spruce 'em up a little before I take them out, but I sell three-quarters of every litter. There's a lot of money in cats, if you do it right. Now, I plan to be gone from the first to the fifteenth. The food is in that cabinet over there, and some fresh litter if you need it. You did say ten dollars a trip, right?"

Lyn told herself it was none of her business. She was not going to get in a brawl with this woman over the ethical treatment of animals. It wasn't her job to tell people how to live their lives, not anymore. She wasn't

going to threaten to call the SPCA, she was not going to
bring in the health department, she was not even going to
tell the woman what she could do with her lousy ten-
dollars-a-visit job. She had heard about places like this,
the puppy and kitten mills that churned out sick, men-
tally unbalanced pets like factory toys, and they were
everywhere. As long as there was a market for the prod-
uct, people like Mrs. Crebs would stay in business, and
there was nothing Lyn could do about it. She couldn't
change the whole damn world, could she?

So she looked at the other woman, forced a sweet
smile, and said, "Yes, that's right. Ten dollars a visit—
per animal."

Mrs. Crebs eyes widened. "But—I have twenty cats!"

"That would come to two hundred dollars a visit,"
agreed Lyn pleasantly. "Every other day for two weeks,
that's—"

"Fourteen hundred dollars!" gasped the other woman.
"That's outrageous! That's the most ridiculous thing I
ever heard! Why, my whole trip to California won't cost
that much!"

"I'm so sorry," Lyn replied innocently, "but that's our
price. You pay for quality, you know."

"But they're just cats!"

Lyn forcefully clamped down on a reply. Smile frozen
in place, she extended her hand. "I'm so sorry we
couldn't do business. I do wish you luck in finding
someone else."

The other woman ignored her hand. "But I'm leaving
tomorrow!"

"I'm sorry," Lyn repeated, and turned toward the
door, walking quickly before she gave in to the temptation to do something she would regret.

The other woman trailed after her, muttering things about "highway robbery" and "there ought to be a law" and with every word Lyn's muscles clenched tighter until only the pressure of her nails against her palms reminded her that there was, indeed, a law against assault and battery—which was doubtless what it would be termed if she were to turn around and slap the formidable Mrs. Crebs.

On the porch she stopped, and the surge of rage caught in her throat as her eyes fell on the dog huddled under the tree. He was a mess. He had no personality, no looks, nothing at all to recommend him to an eager child looking for a playmate. He was malnourished and probably ill. She did not like to think of his chances once he reached the dog pound—if indeed, Mr. Crebs didn't shoot him before he got there.

Maybe she couldn't change the world, but she might be able to do something about the plight of one poor dog. She turned abruptly. "Are you really going to send that dog to the pound?" she demanded. "Because I think I can find a home for him."

Mrs. Crebs's eyes narrowed suspiciously. "I'm not giving him away."

Lyn's nostrils flared with a breath but once more she managed to bite back a retort. "How much?" she inquired stiffly.

The woman did not hesitated. "Twenty dollars."

Lyn opened her purse and took out two tens. She slapped them into the other woman's open hand with a bit more force than was necessary, then marched down the steps toward the dog without another word.

Casey, to Lyn's great relief, was in one of the front exercise yards when she drove up. Two German shepherds were painstakingly working an obstacle course that involved climbing a ladder, crawling through tires, and scaling a wood plank barrier. Lyn watched in amazement for a moment as, under Casey's patient guidance, the two dogs performed feats canines were never meant to accomplish, and then Casey noticed her.

He waved as she got out of the car, and whistled sharply to the dogs. Lyn's own canine passenger, who was huddled on the floorboard between the front and back seats, did not even prick his ears. Casey led the German shepherds out of the exercise area and into another, enclosed play yard, then came over to her.

"Hi," he said.

He was dressed in denim cutoffs and a whale-motif T-shirt, his hair was tousled and his face, already a golden color, showed evidence of the beginnings of a new sunburn. Lyn had not expected the quickening of her pulses when she saw him again, nor had she expected his slow, smiling gaze, as it moved over her, to bring back such vivid memories of his hands on her body, his mouth melding with hers.

She swallowed against a sudden dryness in her throat and replied, "Hi." She leaned against the car door a little self-consciously, then remembered the white culottes she was wearing and stepped away quickly. "I, uh, brought you something," she said, gesturing toward the back seat.

With an inquiring lift of his eyebrow Casey moved around her and looked through the back window.

"Oh, Casey, it was awful," she blurted. "This horrible woman had him tied up to a tree without any food or water and he couldn't even move! They were going to shoot him! And when I offered to take him she had the

nerve to demand twenty dollars for him! Can you believe that? She ought to be arrested."

Casey glanced at her, his eyes twinkling. "Well now,"
he drawled. "Looks like you got yourself a little involved, didn't you? And a dog's a big responsibility."

"Me?" She shook her head adamantly. "Oh, no, not
me. I brought him for you. You said you got most of
your dogs from the pound, and that's where this poor
creature would have ended up—if he'd lived long enough.
You said mutts made the best workers, didn't you? He's
definitely a mutt. I figured you could—" she made a
helpless gesture with her wrist "—do something with
him."

Casey's expression was both dubious and amused as he
stepped away from the door. "Well, get him out here and
let's see what we've got."

Lyn smiled weakly. "Well, that might be a problem..." But she didn't want to explain to Casey how
she'd almost gotten bitten trying to untie the dog, and
how she ended up carrying him to the car in her arms.
She didn't think any of that would make a very good first
impression. So she squared her shoulders and opened the
car door determinedly.

"Come on, dog," she called. "Come on out."

The huddled mass of fur and fleas did not move.

"Here, dog. Come on, pooch—"

"What's his name?" Casey interrupted.

Lyn hesitated. "I don't know. I don't know if he even
has one."

"He needs a name, and you should start using it right
away."

Lyn looked at the bundle of matted black-and-white
fur cowering on the floorboards and decided, "Rabbit.
I'm going to call him Rabbit."

Casey cast her a dry look. "Honey, that dog is going to have to work his way up to having as much spirit as a rabbit."

"I don't care. I had an Easter bunny one time that had those markings, and he kind of reminds me of it. Besides, it's easy to remember."

And because she could see both she and the dog were losing points in Casey's esteem with every moment that was lost, she leaned into the car and demanded, "Come on, Rabbit, stop fooling around. Get out here."

She reached for Rabbit, and he snapped at her. Lyn gave a startled cry and leaped back.

"Don't let him get away with that!"

Casey pushed past her before she could stop him. In another instant he had whipped a choke collar from his pocket and dropped it over the dog's head. With a single jerk he propelled the animal out of the car.

"What are you doing?" Lyn cried. "Be careful!"

"Don't start out by letting a dog get the upper hand. If he knows he can scare you once, you'll never be able to control him."

Casey had attached a short leather handle to the collar and Rabbit was fighting it furiously, growling and tossing his head, his hackles raised. Lyn couldn't believe that he had chosen this moment to start showing some spirit, and she could see a serious dog bite forthcoming.

"It's okay, Casey, let him go. He's just upset, he'll calm down . . ."

Ignoring her, Casey got down on his knees and grasped the ruff of fur on either side of Rabbit's neck with both hands, holding his head steady.

"What are you doing?"

Casey did not reply.

For about thirty seconds Rabbit kept up a low, ominous growling in his throat, but when he tried to turn his head away Casey pulled it back, forcing the dog to meet his eyes. It was the most amazing thing Lyn had ever seen. The growling stopped. After a while, the tail started to wag uncertainly. Several times the dog tried to look away but each time Casey forced his eyes back to him. And after about three minutes of this silent battle of gazes, Rabbit emitted a low, submissive whine and licked Casey's face.

Casey stood up, and Rabbit dropped his head between his paws, his eyes fixed on Casey in an expression that, though not exactly adoring, was certainly respectful. And for the first time he looked like a real dog, rather than that pitiful mound of misused flesh Lyn had first found tied to the tree.

She looked at Casey in amazement. "What are you," she breathed, "some kind of mesmerist?"

He shook his head. "You've got to establish dominance right away, and since I'd probably come off second best in a dog fight, I used the next best thing—staring. Go bring me that leash over on the fence post there, will you?"

Lyn realized that he had the tab of the collar underneath his foot, which was one reason Rabbit hadn't already tried to run away. She hurried to get the leash.

"Then you'll take him?" Lyn said as she returned. "I mean, I know he's not much to look at, but neither is that ugly dog on the beer commercials and—"

Casey laughed softly, shaking his head as he snapped the leash on the collar. "If this dog had the looks of Lassie and heart of Rin-Tin-Tin, he still wouldn't make it to a beer commercial—or anything else. No..." He handed the leash to her. "I figure with a year or so of hard obedience training you might be able to turn him into a house dog—and I say *might*—but there's nothing I can do with him.''

Lyn stared at the leash in her hand, then at the immobile dog on the other end of it. ''But—but you just did do something with him. Look how well behaved he is now—''

He shook his head, grinning. ''That's not good behavior, that's dumb fear. I have to pick my animals carefully, Lyn, and this one just doesn't have what it takes. I'm sorry.''

''But—''

''I'll tell you what,'' he volunteered. ''I'll help you get him cleaned up and give him a quick vet check, then we'll see what we've got. I can't let you take him home like this, at any rate.''

''I can't take him home at all!'' Lyn protested, alarmed.

But Casey had the leash in hand and, once again, she had no choice but to follow him.

Two hours later Lyn was covered with dog hair, splotched with water, and exhausted. She sat beside Casey on his screened back porch while Rabbit, a much cleaner but far more traumatized dog, curled up in a kennel in the sun to dry.

''Why is it,'' she complained, ''that every time I'm around you I end up filthy and wet?''

He grinned and handed her a beer. ''I lead an active life.''

''So I've noticed.''

Lyn closed her eyes, shuddering a little as the vision of all those poor caged kittens came back to her. ''God, Casey, you should have seen it. Those poor kitties—filthy, sick—she didn't even have the decency to give them fresh water! And the smell!'' She shuddered again. "How can people like that be allowed to live? Why doesn't someone *do* something?"

Casey nodded soberly. "I've had a run in or two with the good Mrs. Crebs myself. When a person won't listen to reason there's not much you can do—although I've long been in favor of bringing back public flogging.'' He sipped his beer. "The SPCA has closed her down twice, but never for long. People like that always manage to bounce back.''

"But there's got to be *something* you can do!"

His smile was brief and dry. "Like what? A commando raid to free the kitties?"

Lyn hesitated, but she could not share his smile. "No," she mumbled miserably. "I guess not." It was none of her business anyway. She had saved the dog, hadn't she? That was enough largess for one day on the part of a woman who had made it her credo not to get involved. And look what that had gotten her: one ragtag, fearful, snapping dog who showed his gratitude by growling whenever she came near. And now it was beginning to look as though she was *stuck* with him. No, the cats were definitely none of her business. There was no point in worrying about it for another minute.

Casey was watching her, as though he expected her to say something else. When she didn't, he turned to look back at Rabbit's kennel and commented, "He looks like he might have a little border collie in him."

Lyn looked at him hopefully. "Is that good?"

"It's not bad," he admitted. "But don't get your hopes up. You've heard the expression 'worthless dog'? I think you've got a living example."

It was foolish of Lyn to take insult at that. He wasn't *her* dog, after all. "Didn't I hear somewhere that there are no bad dogs, only bad masters?" Then she shook her head briskly, as though to clear it. "What am I saying? I don't even like dogs!"

"I've got another old saying for you," Casey said. "'You save a dog's life, and you're responsible for it forever.'"

Lyn frowned. "I never heard that one before."

"I read it in a fortune cookie."

"I *can't* take that dog home. I don't even have a home, and Pat would kill me. Casey, are you sure you can't..."

She looked at him hopefully, but he shook his head. "Sorry."

She peeled back the tab of her beer with a vicious gesture. "You are the most stubborn, insensitive man I've ever met," she muttered.

He said, "I'm glad you came over today."

She looked at him and he was smiling at her, a gentle, pervasive smile that caused a tickling in the back of her throat and made her feel warm all over. She lowered her eyes quickly to avoid the power of that smile, but she couldn't stop herself from asking, somewhat huskily, "Why?"

"Because I missed you." He reached across the distance between their two chairs and caught her hand. Her fingers were cold from contact with the beer can, but quickly thawed beneath his warm, callused touch.

"How could you miss me?" She tried to keep her tone playful, but couldn't prevent a small catch in her throat as his index finger traced a titillating pattern along the center of her palm. "You've only known me for a few days."

"I know what I like. But I already told you that, didn't I?"

Lyn didn't know how to respond to that. His words made her feel excited and girlish; her heart started pumping with an irregular rhythm and the warmth of his hand around hers spread with sweet slowness through her veins. But she wasn't a girl; she was a twenty-eight-year-old woman with far too many complications in her life to get involved with this man.

Gently she extracted her hand from his and took a sip of the beer. She said casually, "Rabbit looks a lot better. That shampoo you used really helped. I should pay you for it—and the eye drops, and vitamins."

His tone was as casual as hers. "No charge."

She insisted, "You don't get the medicine free, do you?"

"No," he admitted.

"Then I'll pay."

He lifted the beer can to his lips. "Suit yourself. But it's expensive."

"All the more reason. How much?"

Casey imagined that, in all the history of the world, there had never been a man who worked so hard to get something he did not want. But he couldn't seem to help himself. He didn't want Lyn Sanders in his life, but for the past three days he hadn't been able to think about anything except how to see her again. If she hadn't come over today he would have gone to her, which only proved how ill equipped he was to handle the effect she had on him. Now she was here, and he had no intention of letting the chance slip by.

So he smiled and said, "About three afternoons a week."

"What?"

His expression was perfectly innocent as he looked at her. "I still need some help around here. And you never did give me an answer about that job."

"Oh, for heaven's—!" She broke off in exasperation and set her beer on the plant stand at her elbow. "I *gave* you an answer—no, remember? Or isn't that word in your vocabulary?"

"As a matter of fact, I'm very familiar with that word. And if I weren't, I would have learned all I need to know about it since I met you."

"Then why do you keep asking me to work for you? There must be lots of more qualified—or at least willing—people you could get. Why me?"

"Reduced to its simplest terms?" He appeared to think about that for a moment. "Because it's an obvious solution to a clear problem. You need something to do, I've got something that needs doing."

"I don't—" she interrupted, but he held up a hand for silence.

"And because," he added, "I want to see more of you." His eyes met hers with quiet honesty, stripping away the power of her retort. "My life is crowded, Lyn. I've been working since five-thirty this morning and I'll still be working at eleven-thirty tonight . . . which doesn't leave much time left over for a social life. A lot of living things depend on me and I can't just put them on hold because a woman with big gray eyes and curly red hair sweeps me off my feet, now can I?"

She fought the smile he was trying to coax from her. "So it's like killing two birds with one stone?"

He winced. "I guess I have to admit that's not the most romantic thing I've ever said."

"I certainly hope not."

Then he was serious again. "I don't want to hire you, Lyn. I just want to be with you. If this doesn't work, I'll think of something else. But I won't give up."

It was risky, saying that to her, even admitting it to himself. He couldn't believe he had done it. Would she understand what he was really offering her? A relationship with limits, no promises, nothing serious. Definitely nothing serious. But Lyn didn't want a heavy involvement any more than he did; of course she understood.

After all, she would be leaving soon. They both knew exactly what to expect from each other.

She stood and walked toward the edge of the porch to hide the smile that had finally broken through. "If that was Plan A," she murmured, "I'm not sure I want to know what Plan B is."

"Does that mean you accept?"

She clasped her hands behind her back, looking at Rabbit, who was sleeping peacefully in the safety of his wire kennel. "Maybe," she mused, "if I could get him spruced up, and teach him a few tricks, someone might want to adopt him. Maybe you could help me."

"Maybe," he agreed, albeit cautiously.

"Of course, I'd have to do it before Pat got home."

"That I can't promise you."

She said, "Do I really sweep you off your feet?"

She turned cautiously, not knowing quite what to expect. He was smiling, and he extended his hands to her. "Yes," he said softly. "You sweep me off my feet. Come here."

She hesitated, then put her hands in his. He drew her close, with a gentle insistent pressure, until she was standing between his knees. Then he lifted his hands to her hips and urged her downward to sit on his thigh. His eyes were close, summer-soft, as deep as a hidden forest glade. She understood his mesmeric power over animals. His essence went through her in hypnotic waves, and he held her captive.

He said, "Why are you fighting this so hard, Lyn? Why can't you just relax and let things happen?"

She didn't know whether he meant the job, or the relationship. She thought he meant both. And she thought he also knew the answer—because it wasn't just a job that she didn't need and didn't want. It wasn't just seeing him two or three times a week, playing with the animals and getting dirty. It was a relationship. He had managed to make it a package deal, and that was what she had known from the beginning. *That* was what she was fighting.

She rested her hands on his arms, dropping her eyes. "Because," she said, "I'm not—good at this. I don't seem to be able to do anything right lately, everything I touch turns to mud. This whole thing is a bad idea, and you're going to be sorry you ever asked me."

His hand stroked her back lightly, sweet, soothing caresses that melted through her muscles. He answered softly, "I'm hardly ever sorry about anything I do."

She lifted her eyes to him, her voice barely above a whisper. "Because you're always right?"

He smiled. "Because I'm always certain."

And now he was certain. This was going to be good, for both of them.

His hands slid up her spine and cupped her neck. By inches his eyes grew closer until they filled her entire vision. His breath warmed her cheek. His lips brushed hers, tasted, released, and tasted again. His mouth covered hers, and she sank into his kiss.

Every fiber in her body seemed to dissolve into him. Distant sounds faded into one glorious rush of pulsing whispers, lights and shadows strobed behind her closed eyes. His hands were strong upon her back, caressing the shape of her hip, tightening on her thigh. She drank of him, inhaling his heat and his taste, drowning in the strength and the solidity and the certainty that was Casey. How easy it would be to lose herself in him. How beautifully, terrifyingly easy...

And yet he did not press; he did not insist. The kiss ended softly, reluctantly, and he moved his hands lightly to her waist.

Lyn's arms were looped around his neck; she dropped her forehead to his shoulder, struggling to moderate her breathing. She said after a moment, "Why—did you do that? You shouldn't... keep doing that."

She felt, rather than saw, his smile. "Then tell me to stop."

But she couldn't. He knew she couldn't. There was something between them, a chemistry she couldn't explain, and once it was ignited was not easily extinguished. She shouldn't have come here today. She should go home now and forget this had ever happened. She should most certainly never see him again.

She stiffened her elbows in preparation for rising, and sat up straight. Her voice was only a little shaky. "I'm going home now."

He guided her to her feet, and stood beside her. "Will I see you tomorrow?"

She opened her mouth to say no, but ended up nodding her head affirmatively.

He smiled, stroking her cheek. "Good."

"No. It's not good." She took a breath, and released it in a helpless sigh. "Oh, Casey. I think you're the worst thing that could have happened to me."

He threaded his fingers through her hair, and he bent to kiss her cheek. The gentle warmth of his eyes fell over her like sunshine as he suggested, "Or the best."

After a moment, she managed a weak smile. She wished she could believe that. But she didn't.

Six

It was a quarter till eleven two nights later when Lyn marched up the steps to Casey's house and knocked firmly on the door. Her palms were sweaty and her throat was dry but she did not back down. It had taken her two days to work up the courage; two days of fuming and fretting and two nights of lying awake wrestling with her conscience and she was not going to put herself through that anymore. Tonight, for better or worse, she was taking a stand.

Casey's lights were still on, and it didn't take him long to answer the door.

"How much money do you have?" she demanded abruptly.

His first surprised welcome faded into a twinkle of amusement, and he leaned back against the doorjamb, folding his arms. "And here I was thinking all this time it was my body you wanted."

Lyn was too agitated to respond to that, though at another time she might have been tempted. He was in his bare feet, wearing denim shorts and a short-sleeved shirt that was unbuttoned over his bare chest. Lyn could have spent a great deal of time looking at that leanly muscled, tanned chest with the intriguing pattern of light hair that spread across his breast muscles, but she forcefully jerked her eyes away. She couldn't get sidetracked now. She couldn't afford to lose her nerve.

She repeated, "How much?"

The amusement in his eyes became mitigated with curiosity. "Not enough, I'll bet. Would you like to come in and tell me why you ask?"

Lyn strode past him and into the living room. A cat pounced playfully at her shoes and she picked it up, holding it briefly against her cheek. Any possibility of losing her resolve was gone then, just as she knew it would be. She felt stronger, just being here.

She turned back to Casey, "I'm going to go over to Mrs. Crebs's house and free those kittens," she told him, holding the cat against her chest defiantly. "It's what somebody should have done a long time ago." And, at his slightly lifted eyebrow she rushed on, "I've been calling her all day and she's gone, Casey. I'll bet you everything I own she didn't find anybody to take care of those poor animals—she just probably filled a trough with cat food and left them. Why should she care if half of them are dead when she gets back—she's got nothing invested in them! So I figured if something's going to be done it's got to be now, while she's away, and while the cats still have a chance."

The amusement in his eyes would have been maddening if Lyn had not been so worked up by her own passion she didn't care. He said, "I thought you weren't going to get involved."

She was holding the cat against her chest too tightly, and it squirmed to be let down. She defended, "Animals are different. They can't take care of themselves. And besides...oh, what difference does it make? You were right, okay? I can't *not* get involved!"

She expected more teasing, and she probably deserved it. But Casey merely smiled and said, "Good for you." Then, "So where does the money come in?"

This was the embarrassing part. "Well, I didn't want to be accused of stealing, so I thought if I left her some money it wouldn't technically be theft...all she cares about is money anyway. But," she admitted, "I only have about seventy-five dollars, and that's not very much, is it, for twenty purebred cats? So I thought if you could..."

She trailed off, realizing how absurd the whole thing sounded. "Never mind," she said, "it's a crazy idea. I mean, this isn't your problem and I understand if you don't want to get involved. But I really would appreciate the use of your van for a couple of hours."

He looked at her thoughtfully. "You could use more than that."

"Like common sense?"

"Like a good lawyer. You do realize of course that what you're planning is breaking and entering, and last I heard that was against the law. What if you get caught?"

Lyn swallowed hard. Did he think she hadn't thought of that? Did he think she wasn't scared to death? But she met his eyes boldly and replied, "I'll just have to be careful not to get caught."

Casey looked at her for a long moment. "And you want me to drive the getaway car?"

She exclaimed, "Oh, Casey, would you?"

A rueful smile tugged his lips. "Well, it wouldn't be very chivalrous of me to let you go to jail by yourself, would it?"

"Oh, Casey, I knew you'd understand! Thank you!"

"Don't thank me yet. So far all I've done is agree to help you commit a felony. Hold on, let me get my shoes."

"Casey?"

He turned back.

She said hesitantly, "What about the money?"

He made a dismissing gesture. "Forget that. I've got something better."

"What?"

He grinned and tossed over his shoulder, "Influence."

They made one stop before Mrs. Crebs's house, and when Lyn questioned him, Casey replied only that he had to "see an old friend for a minute." He returned less than five minutes later and offered no further explanation, and Lyn, whose anxiety level had risen almost beyond tolerance point, didn't pry. She only wanted to get this over with.

They pulled up on the quiet neighborhood street that ran in front of the Crebses' house, and Casey, with typical brashness, parked right beneath a street light. Lyn looked around nervously. "Don't you think it would be better if we picked a darker spot?"

"We've got to be able to see what we're doing," Casey reminded her. He made no effort to muffle the slamming of the van door as he got out. "There's no point in rescuing the cats if we just lose them in the dark."

Lyn had to concede the logic in that, but she shushed him loudly as he flung open the back of the van and began rummaging around between the animal cages, making a great deal of noise. "Do you want the neighbors to hear us? Someone's going to call the police!"

Casey brought out a sturdy crowbar and Lyn looked at it in dismay. Until that moment she had given very little thought to exactly *how* they were going to get into the house. "I was kind of hoping," she ventured, "after the way you opened my car door...well, that you knew something about jimmying house locks, too."

He shrugged. "Why waste the time?"

She was growing alarmed. "But—I don't have a key, and I didn't really want to do any damage."

He looked at her patiently. "Look, you can't just politely break into someone's house and steal their property. Now, if you want to call it off..."

For just a moment Lyn wavered. She looked uneasily around to the neighbors' houses, then up the dark driveway to their intended target. She, Lyn Sanders, a common criminal. But if she cared enough about something to right a wrong, she cared enough to accept the consequences. And she *did* care. It had been a long time since she'd felt this kind of passionate commitment to a cause stir inside her, and it was a little frightening. But it was also thrilling.

She met Casey's eyes and shook her head firmly. "No," she said, "I don't want to call it off."

He reached forward and slipped his fingers behind her neck. Drawing her to him, he kissed her hard on the lips. Lyn barely had time to catch her breath before he released her, and she stumbled back a little, staring at him.

"That," he told her softly, "was in respect and admiration. And this..." He reached into his back pocket and brought out a folded paper, "is an impound warrant. It gives us full legal authority to search for and seize any animals we find on the premises that we suspect of being abused." He grinned. "One of the few advantages of being a past president of the Humane Society—connections."

She didn't know whether to hug him or to shake him. "But I thought you said there was nothing we could do!"

"No," he corrected. "I said I'd already tried. I guess," he admitted, "I just needed to be reminded it couldn't hurt to try again."

Then Lyn did hug him, and in the strong warmth of their embrace something tender and tenuous formed between them, a moment of recognition, of cautious truth, of wondrous certainty. Something changed, between and within them; it was wonderful and it was frightening, and it was too new for either of them to examine closely yet.

Casey stepped away first. He said, smiling, "What are we waiting for?" And they went together to the house.

"I can't do this anymore," Lyn announced, and sat down firmly on the ground. "It's cruel and inhumane and I'm not going to be a part of it."

"Thus speaks the expert in animal behavior," Casey teased her, and she scowled.

Since the "cat caper"—as Casey never tired of referring to it—he was relentless with his quips, and Lyn supposed most of it was deserved. She had made a decision, she had done something positive, and maybe it was just a little thing and maybe it had gone to her head, but she had a right to be proud of herself. Twenty cats now had a chance to find good homes through the Humane Society, and some of them would even be auctioned off for donations to help support the Society's other work. An evil woman had been put out of business. Lyn had made a difference. She was a lot more confident now than she had been when he first met her, and not afraid to express her opinion. If sometimes those opinions clashed with Casey's, that was too bad. He was the one, after all, who had insisted that she work with him.

For the past half hour her job had been to tempt, harass and otherwise torment an eighteen-month-old black Lab called Samson while Casey put the dog through a series of behaviors that ranged from simple obedience to complex performance tricks. While Samson was in a down-stay she crept up behind him and banged on tin pie plates or called to him from a distance; when he was given a command to retrieve a pair of car keys she tossed sticks and toys in the opposite direction; most recently she had followed along beside him, tempting Samson to break the heel position with a dog biscuit held a few inches in front of his nose. Each time she was successful in distracting the dog—each time he hesitated over a command, sniffed at the biscuit, or in fact even looked at it—Casey would correct him with a snap of the leash and a shout so angry it hurt Lyn's ears. She knew it wasn't her place to tell Casey how to do his job, but this, she was certain, was going beyond the bounds of what was necessary.

She repeated, "It's cruel, and I'm not going to be responsible for damaging that poor dog's psyche."

Casey stopped before her and Samson dropped immediately into a sitting position at Casey's knee. "Cruel?" he questioned mildly. "No, honey, what would be cruel is if this dog allowed himself to be distracted while he was guiding a blind person and walked right out into the middle of traffic. Now, come on, get back to work."

Lyn shook her head. "That's not the point. You treat all your dogs this way—not just the ones that are going to end up being guide dogs. Besides, no one is going to follow this dog down the street while he's working and wave a dog biscuit under his nose. *That's* cruel—to offer a dog a treat and then punish him for trying to take it."

Casey nodded thoughtfully. "Well, that's true. It's also cruel to send a child out in the world where there are drug pushers on every corner and smooth-talking people in strange cars offering them candy, isn't it? But parents do it every day because, hopefully at least, they've taught their kids how to say no."

Lyn frowned uncomfortably. "That's not the same."

"It's exactly the same. Discipline, self-control—they build character. You work to get to the point where the dog doesn't make a single move without thinking about his master—just like a child should measure everything he does against the standards of right and wrong he's been taught."

"But that's just the point!" Lyn exclaimed. "You're talking about total control, you can't do that with people and you shouldn't do that with animals—it's just not right. They were meant to be wild, and free...and I don't like to see them turned into robots."

Casey dropped the leash and sat down on the grass across from Lyn, drawing up his legs Indian style. Samson, even though he was no longer controlled by the leash, remained exactly where he was and never took his eyes off Casey.

"All right," he agreed reasonably, "let's take a pack of dogs in the wild. The way they were meant to be, right? The first thing a new pup learns is how to live with the pack—and dogs have a much less tolerant society than we do. If dog can't learn to obey the rules, or accept the authority of the leader, he's driven out to fend for himself, where he'll end up being chased down and eaten by someone who *does* know what the rules are. Now, the worst that can happen to a dog when he comes to live in *my* pack is that he gets yelled at a few times. Given the alternative, which is crueler?''

The one thing Lyn had discovered—and learned to dislike intensely—over the past few days of working with Casey was that it was impossible to outmaneuver him in a debate. He was always reasonable, always patient, and always right.

"Without discipline," Casey pointed out mildly, "and a sense of control over your environment, there is no freedom. It's as simple as that."

The other thing she had learned to dislike was his uncanny ability to turn almost any abstract point into a personal one. Sometimes Lyn felt as though she were the one in training, not the dogs.

She said, "I still don't see why you have to be so mean. Why can't you just teach your animals to do what you want them to because they love you?"

His eyes twinkled. "How's Rabbit doing?"

Lyn scowled. Casey knew very well how Rabbit was doing. He was tied to the porch on a long lead because he ran every time Lyn approached him. After three days he was no closer to being housebroken than he had been the first day Lyn brought him home, and she still hadn't the courage to tell Pat about their new acquisition. He spent most of his time eating or hiding under the dining-room table—when he wasn't chewing up eighty-dollar running shoes or snarling at the postman—and, though she showered him with affection and bribed him with treats, Lyn could not even teach him to come when he was called. And that, despite her success with the cat caper, did absolutely nothing to bolster Lyn's self-confidence.

Most insulting of all, Rabbit adored Casey. He didn't know his own name, but his ears pricked up when he heard Casey's. When Casey told him to sit, he almost tripped over himself in his eagerness to comply. When Lyn told him to sit he generally walked off someplace to take a nap.

It was control, Lyn decided. That sense of confidence and power Casey exuded was irresistible to all weak-spirited things...like Rabbit, like herself. It wasn't right, it wasn't honest, but it was nonetheless irrefutable.

She said, "I need to get home. Pat's due in late tomorrow and I've got a lot of house cleaning to do."

He chuckled and glanced at Rabbit, who was snoozing beneath the shade of the porch. "I'll bet you do."

But as she started to rise he placed his hands lightly on her bare legs. It was a casual touch that held no intimacy or suggestion behind it, just a gentle pressure on her knees, gesturing her to stay. But the touch went through her like a low-voltage electric current, thrumming through nerve endings and heating her senses, and she looked at him, startled.

Since that night in front of Mrs. Crebs's house, Casey had very carefully, very deliberately kept their relationship on a semi-impersonal basis. There had been no searing kisses, no long meaningful looks, no stolen caresses. She had been both grateful and conversely confused by that. She had even hoped that the long hours of arguing and sweaty, undignified work had made her immune to the chemistry of his presence, and was surprised and dismayed to find that nothing could be further from the truth.

But if Casey was aware of the effect his simple touch had on her he did not show it. His tone was conversational as he said, "You remember that movie I was doing with Sheba?"

She smiled weakly as his hands drifted from her knees to rest behind him on the ground again. "How could I forget?" She had the rare pleasure of helping Casey put Sheba through her paces twice this week, and nothing about the giant cat was forgettable.

"We're going into town to finish up next week. I thought you might like to come with me. It'll be an overnight stay," he added, almost too casually.

Already, Lynn's heart was beating faster than normal, though she could read nothing on his face beyond the friendly, matter-of-fact invitation. What was he suggesting? Why was he suggesting it?

"I thought you might enjoy being on the set," he added easily. "And if we get finished in time we could take in some of the attractions—even stay the weekend, if you like."

Casey wasn't fooling himself any more than he was her, and he didn't know why he even tried. The truth was, she was becoming an obsession with him, a fever in his blood, and the more he tried to deny it the worse it became. She was getting to him, affecting him on a level that was far deeper than sexual…like that business with the cats. Why had he done that? It was crazy, it was quixotic, and it was not like him at all. But something in Lyn had touched something in him and all of a sudden he was involved. That disturbed him deeply, and the only thing he knew to do about it was to get this relationship back on course, to carry it to its natural conclusion. To get her out of his system. A working weekend on the movie set? He knew better than that, and so did she.

Lyn cleared her throat. She couldn't believe she had considered it, even for a moment. "Um, thanks, but I don't think so. I mean, who'll take care of your animals while you're gone, and there's Rabbit—"

"I thought you said Pat was coming home tomorrow."

"She is, but that doesn't mean she wants to go to work right away. Besides, I haven't seen her in so long and she doesn't even *know* about Rabbit. I can't just run off and leave her."

Casey said, "I hired a kid to do the kennel work this morning. He'll be more than capable of feeding the animals. You can even leave Rabbit here if you don't feel like saddling Pat with him. It's only for two days, you know. I think Pat would understand if you took a forty-eight-hour furlough."

Lyn leaned back on her palms in what she hoped was a casual gesture, letting her eyes wander over the yard until they rested at last on Samson, who was still sitting attentively where Casey had left him.

"Why don't you let that poor dog lie down?" she said.

"Why don't you give me an answer?" But he turned and made a hand gesture to the dog; Samson, with a huff of relief, lay down and put his head between his paws.

Lyn met his eyes. "Why do you want me along?"

He smiled. "Because, my dear, I'm tired of lying awake at night wishing you were in my arms. Because I have visions of sweeping you away to some luxurious resort with pictures of cartoon characters on the walls and making love to you into the wee hours of the morning. Because we can't go on pretending forever."

Lyn could not tell whether he was serious, but it didn't matter. His voice, soft and husky, went through her like a liquid shiver and his words conjured up visions that left her weak.

She said, as steadily as she could, "I take my cartoons very seriously."

His smile was gentle and a little sad. "How much longer are you going to keep saying no to life?"

"No is a good word." She got to her feet. "It teaches discipline and builds character."

He stood beside her. "How about dinner tonight?"

That really surprised her. "What?"

"Dinner?" he repeated. "That meal that comes between lunch and bedtime? Sometimes eaten in restaurants on social occasions, like when a man wants to impress a woman he's very interested in?"

"Do you mean—a date?"

His smile was rueful. "Well, I've tried everything else. Why not a date? Surely you can't find any reason to object to that."

The trouble was, Lyn couldn't find any reason to object. Even worse, she wanted to accept. She wanted to get dressed up for him, to spend an evening talking about things men and women talked about on dates, to have fun. And the realization shocked her so much that, before she knew it she was saying, "Thanks. I'd like that."

He looked as surprised as she was for a moment, then he smiled. "Great. I think I can get things straightened out around here by six. Is that too early?"

"No. That's fine. I—I'll see you then."

She was in such a state of confusion that she almost forgot Rabbit, and it took another five minutes to coax him into the car. Casey was laughing as she drove away, but Lyn barely noticed. She was already beginning to suspect she had made a mistake, and all the way home kept herself busy making up excuses to cancel.

* * *

The telephone was ringing when Lyn arrived home. Dragging on Rabbit's leash, struggling to get the key in the lock, she reached the telephone just as the answering machine picked up. She grimaced at the telephone and unfastened Rabbit's leash, then had to tug on his collar to get him out the patio door while the answering machine message played in the background.

"Come on, you mangy mutt, outside. I don't know what I was thinking about, telling him I'd go out tonight. I've got to clean the house and wash my hair and anyway, what would I do with you? Pat wouldn't have a house left if I went out and left you alone!"

And then she heard Pat's voice on the answering machine speaker.

Lyn shoved Rabbit through the patio door and raced to pick up the receiver. "Hi, Pat!" She was a little breathless. "Don't hang up, I'm here."

"What, you're not out making money for me while I'm gone?"

Pat sounded cheerful and relaxed, as she had every time she had called from North Carolina. Lyn was glad the vacation had been as wonderful as Pat had expected it to be, even though her sister's absence had complicated her own life more than she wanted to tell.

"Sorry, business has been a little slow."

"You sound like you just got in."

"Well . . . I did. I was over at Casey's."

Lyn had made the mistake of mentioning, in the most offhanded way, Casey Carmichael and his job offer, and of course Pat had read far too much between the lines . . . or perhaps she had read exactly what had transpired between the two of them.

"And?" her sister prompted eagerly.

"And he made me jump through hoops and climb tall buildings and fetch sticks from the middle of a lake, the same old stuff. And he asked me out to dinner tonight," she added without meaning to.

Pat practically chortled with glee. "I knew it! I told Marilee only last night . . . well, let's have some details! He's adorable, isn't he? Didn't I tell you he was? And perfect for you. I mean you both have the same kind of background—sociology, psychology, that sort of thing, and—"

"Oh, for heaven's sake, Pat, we're not going to the altar, just to dinner. And besides, we'll have plenty of time to talk tomorrow. What time are you getting in?"

There was a long pause. "Actually," Pat said, "that's what I called to talk to you about . . ."

"What?" Something in her sister's tone caused alarm signals to go off. "Are you going to be late? Is anything wrong?"

"No," Pat replied quickly, "No, nothing's wrong at all, in fact, everything couldn't be more right. It's just that—well, I've had a little accident, and—"

"*What?* Where are you? What happened? How bad—"

"Hush, stop screeching in my ear. Now calm down and listen to me—are you listening?"

"Yes," Lyn said. She was breathing fast and pacing back and forth to the end of the telephone cord, but she tried not to let her agitation show in her voice. She didn't want to upset Pat any more than she was already. "Yes, I'm listening. Just tell me what hospital you're in and I can be there in—"

Pat's laugh was high and breathless, more like a giggle than the low-pitched, throaty laughter that Lyn usually expected from her sister. "Hospital? Good heavens, far from it. I just twisted my ankle, nothing is even broken. The only thing is, I'm going to have to stay off my feet for a while and the doctor doesn't really think it's a good idea for me to drive back anytime soon. So it looks like I might be here a while.''

Lyn was confused. ''Do you mean—just lying around in the ski lodge while your ankle heals? At those prices? Can't Marilee drive? Do you want me to—''

''No, I don't want you to drive up here and bring me home,'' Pat said, and her voice held more than a hint of exasperation. ''As a matter of fact, I'm sending Marilee home tomorrow with my car. I'll fly home later. And I won't exactly be at the ski lodge. I, um, met someone.''

Lyn wasn't really that naive; she just wasn't accustomed to thinking of her sister in those terms and it took her a moment to catch on. ''What do you mean, someone? Who? And what does that have to do with...'' At last, it dawned on her. ''Oh,'' she said, and sat down abruptly. ''You mean a man.''

''As a matter of fact, it's the same doctor who took care of my ankle, and he's invited me to stay at his condo while I recuperate.'' She must have heard Lyn's gasp, because she explained impatiently, ''No, I didn't just meet him today. We've been on the slopes together all week and had dinner almost every night and...'' Her tone changed, becoming softer, almost dreamy. ''He's really wonderful, Lynnie. I never thought at my age...'' She laughed again, a little self-consciously. ''Even Marilee approves, and you know how picky she is! I wouldn't be a bit surprised if she didn't push me into that other skier just to give me an excuse to stay with him a little longer.''

Lyn was too stunned to say anything, and Pat must have mistaken her silence for disapproval. Her tone was half-defensive, half-pleading as she went on, ''All right, so I don't really have to stay here. I *could* get in the car now and it wouldn't cripple me permanently. But I've been sitting here all day, Lyn, trying to think of reasons why I *shouldn't* stay, and the truth is, you can spend your whole life making up excuses to turn down the good things that come your way and pretty soon...there are no more good things.''

She took a small breath, and Lyn could picture her on the other end of the connection, running her hand through her hair the way she did when she was tense, or uncertain, or trying to sort things out in her mind. "Since Jack died," she said, "I've been—hiding. Making up excuses, trying to protect myself, I guess. And that's stupid, Lynnie. What was I afraid of? Making a mistake? Being hurt? I don't know," she sighed. "Maybe I'm crazy. But this...this could be real. It *feels* real. And I've got to find out. I can't keep hiding any longer.''

It was a long time before Lyn could answer. Her head was spinning, she felt as though she had been knocked off her feet. So many new concepts, new ideas, possibilities...and somehow, wrapped up in all the surprise and confusion over her sister's behavior, Lyn felt as though there was something very important for her.

Unexpectedly she felt tears prick her eyes as she said, ''I'm so happy for you, Pat. I wish I were there now so I could give you a big hug.''

She heard Pat's breath of relief. "Oh, Lyn, do you mean it? Do you think I'm doing the right thing?''

"Absolutely," Lyn said with conviction. "I hope it works out, but even if it doesn't...I think you should stay.''

"Thank you," Pat said softly. "You're the best little sister I ever had.''

Lyn laughed, and Rabbit chose that moment to bark, quite loudly, at the patio door. Lyn covered the receiver, but too late.

"What's that? Did the neighbors get a new dog?"

Lyn glanced anxiously at the door, and said, "Well, actually, I've been meaning to talk to you about that..."

"It doesn't matter," Pat said breezily. "We'll talk when I get back. It may be a couple of weeks longer, are you sure that's okay? You don't mind taking care of things for a while?"

"Are you kidding? What's to take care of? I'm having a great time."

"Because if it's too much, I can—"

"No," Lyn said quickly as Rabbit barked again. "No, don't be silly. You stay as long as you like, I mean it. Don't hurry home."

"You *are* sweet. I don't know what I would do without you, you know that?"

"Just enjoy yourself, and don't worry about a thing."

"I will, I promise. And you have a good time with Casey tonight. I'll call you in a couple of days. I love you."

"Me, too."

Lyn still felt a little stunned as she hung up the phone and went to let Rabbit in. Pat, of all people...she had never expected this from Pat. But she had been a widow for almost eight years now; she was still a young woman and there was no reason for her to spend her life alone. Pat was right, hiding from life was foolish and wasteful.

And if that were true for Pat, wasn't it also true for her sister? The question took Lyn by surprise, and she wasn't entirely sure she wanted to answer it just then. But she did know she was no longer trying to think of excuses to get out of her date with Casey tonight.

She smiled suddenly and her step was light as she started toward the bedroom. "Come on, Rabbit, we've got to get moving. I've only got a couple of hours to get ready for my date."

Rabbit looked at her for a moment, then jumped up on Pat's chintz sofa and settled down to sleep.

Seven

Lyn had bought one dress since coming to Florida: a white gauze with puffy three-quarter-length sleeves, a scooped neck and dropped waist. Tiny buttons fastened with fabric loops all the way up the front, and the neckline and sleeves were trimmed with a delicate row of eyelet lace. She had not worn it since buying it, and was not even sure why she had purchased it, except that when she spotted the dress in an upscale resort-wear shop it had reminded her of one of those perfume ads and she had imagined herself walking down the beach barefoot with the breeze blowing the sheer gauze around her legs and moonlight streaming through her hair...and when she pictured herself wearing it she was beautiful, carefree and content.

She might never be beautiful, but the dress was every bit as flattering as its exorbitant price tag had promised it would be. The long waist molded her slim figure and emphasized the roundness of her breasts, while the scooped neckline somehow managed to soften her shoulders and make her height look less angular. The lavishly full skirt fell just below her calves and clung to her legs when she moved, making her feel feminine and romantic. She took advantage of her curly hair by pulling it up and away from her face with mother-of-pearl combs, letting it just graze the back of her shoulders in wispy strands. She didn't want the transformation to be so dramatic that Casey wouldn't recognize her, so she used the makeup brush sparingly, darkening her lashes with mascara and applying just enough blush and peach lip gloss to give her face color.

Casey was ten minutes early, so she didn't have time for long critical looks in the mirror or second thoughts. When, a little breathless and flushed from wrestling the dog out of her way, she opened the door and saw the look in Casey's eyes she knew second thoughts were not necessary.

He looked different, too, in a blazer and tan trousers, with the top button of his shirt casually open at the throat. His hair was brushed away from his forehead, but little effort had been made to tame the curls, and in the dying sun it seemed to be fringed with gold. His eyes, as they went over her, lightened and darkened with appreciation and surprise and she knew he meant it when he said softly, "You look lovely."

Rabbit had stopped growling and lunging as soon as he recognized Casey, so Lyn released his collar and straightened up. She could feel color tingle in her cheeks as she looked at him—the warmth of pleasure, and excitement, and nervous delight—like a woman going on a first date.

"Thank you," she replied. "You do, too. Do you want to come in, or should we leave?"

He glanced at his watch. "We should probably get started. Do you have a jacket?"

She turned back into the room for Pat's jacket—a white silk blouson style that Lyn hoped fervently her sister would not mind her borrowing. "Where are we going?"

"A place called Quinlin's."

"I don't think I've heard of it."

"That's because it's at the beach."

"The beach?" She turned, staring at him. "But we're nowhere near the beach!"

"It's just a little over an hour's drive away." And then he grinned. "Hey, when I start out to impress a woman, I go all the way."

"I should say so," she murmured, her eyes sparkling with delight. She should have known; an evening with Casey would not be just a date, it would be an adventure.

Then she looked at Rabbit, and her spirits fell. He was sitting before Casey, his tail swishing back and forth along the floor, watching his idol expectantly. A model of behavior now, but as soon as they left the house . . .

"I don't know, Casey," she said reluctantly. "I hadn't expected to be gone that long, and Rabbit . . ."

"No problem," Casey said. "Bring him along."

"While we have dinner? Are you sure?"

"He won't be any trouble at all," Casey promised her. "But . . ." He leaned down and spoke to Rabbit sternly. "You have to sit in the back seat, and no moving in on my girl."

Lyn laughed, but mostly from the unexpected thrill that went through her at being referred to as "his girl."

There were advantages to a long drive to dinner that
Lyn had never imagined before. There was something
about the isolated enclosure of the car and the long miles
of flat Florida landscape disappearing behind them that
encouraged conversation, and a kind of intimacy they
had never shared before. Casey told her about his child-
hood, the trauma of losing his parents at the age of thir-
teen, of the following years on his grandmother's farm.
He did not try to make the stories amusing or introspec-
tive, but she saw the loneliness of a young boy growing
up on an isolated farm with no friends his own age,
turning to animals for companionship. She saw the pain
he felt when he lost his last living relative, and then, only
a few years later, his fiancée. She understood him, quietly
and completely. But she could not help wondering
whether Casey understood himself half as well.

He encouraged her to talk about herself and for the
first time she did not feel inhibited about doing so. Because he, too, had lost his parents at an early age, he
understood about growing up without an anchor. She
told him about Pat, and a lifetime spent torn between resigned jealousy and unquestioned adoration of her older
sister. She even went on to tell him about Pat's reason for
staying longer in North Carolina, and for a while they
discussed the pros, cons, and possible outcomes of Pat's
new relationship. It felt strange to be discussing family
matters with an outsider, but at the same time comfortable. Lyn had never known anyone except her sister with
whom she could talk about things of consequence, and
it was good to have a friend.

Perhaps the most significant thing that happened on
that drive to the beach was that she began to think of
Casey as a friend.

The sun was down by the time the citrus groves gave way to sea grass and sand. The twilight was a rich, deep purple, and the humidity of the day had been swept away by a pleasantly cool breeze that smelled of salt. Casey parked the car in front of a rambling building whose aged plank facade was deceptively rustic; from the number of foreign luxury cars parked in the lot, the restaurant was not only extremely popular, but very upscale.

Rabbit, whose distrust of automobiles was still so intense that he spent most of his time trying to squeeze himself underneath the back seat, had been so quiet on the drive up that Lyn had almost forgotten about him. When Casey stopped the car, however, and walked around to help Lyn out, the dog made a lunge for the door and it took both of them to wrestle him back inside.

When the door was closed, Rabbit began jumping from one window to the other, scratching hysterically at the glass and barking in a wild, high-pitched screech that made Lyn want to cover her ears and slink away in embarrassment.

"Oh, Casey, what are we going to do?" She glanced around anxiously. "We can't leave him here while we eat. He'll tear up your car. Or someone will report us for cruelty to animals. We can't go inside and leave him here."

"Well, I can't say that I blame him," Casey agreed. "I wouldn't want to be locked in a car for two hours, either. I guess we'll just have to take him with us."

"What? Inside the restaurant? Are you crazy?"

"Leave it to me," he assured her.

He opened the car again and reached inside the glove compartment. When he brought Rabbit out on his leash, the dog was sporting a bright yellow cape on which was inscribed the words "Guide Dog in Training."

Lyn looked at Rabbit, who was dashing around Casey's ankles, sniffing the ground with total oblivion to his promotion to the elevated rank of guide dog, and then at Casey. Her tone was dubious. "No one is going to believe he's a guide dog. And no one is going to believe you're blind."

Casey chuckled. "Trust me. I didn't drive an hour for seafood just to have my dinner spoiled by a canine terrorist."

With a sharp jerk on the leash, Casey brought Rabbit to a semiheel, and the dog was so overwhelmed by the sights and sounds of his new environment that he walked more or less obediently beside Casey toward the restaurant. "Just act like you know what you're doing," Casey advised Lyn, and Lyn plastered a fake smile on her face and tried to stop glancing around nervously every time someone looked their way.

The restaurant was divided into indoor and outdoor sections, and the maître d's stand was outside. When Casey gave his name and their reservation time, the maître d' took one look at him and replied, just as Lyn had expected, "I'm sorry, sir, dogs are not allowed in the restaurant."

"That's okay," Casey replied pleasantly. "We prefer to sit outside anyway. That table over there, overlooking the ocean, will be fine."

The maître d' cleared his throat. "What I meant, sir, is that this is a food service establishment. Health laws do not permit pets under any circumstances."

Casey nodded thoughtfully. "I understand. We'll leave if you ask us to, of course, but you should know that the law also provides that guide dogs cannot be denied access to any public building—including restaurants.''

The maître d' looked over the stand, noticed the yellow cape, and registered momentary confusion. "I didn't realize. I don't know...I guess it would be all right.'' He looked over his shoulder as though seeking information from a superior, but finding no one in sight, finally shrugged his shoulders. "Come with me, please.''

Lyn did not release her breath until they were seated, menus in hand, with Rabbit lying quietly and unobtrusively under the table. "I don't believe it,'' she said, sinking back into the chair. "The things you get away with...''

Casey shrugged. "It is a law, you know. And the dog's not bothering anybody.''

"And that's another thing!'' Lyn exclaimed softly. "He's not running wild, he's not growling at people—he's just lying there, acting like a trained dog! How do you do it?''

Casey opened his menu. "For one thing, it's culture shock. He's too scared to leave my side. For another...'' He flashed a grin at her. "I've got my foot on his leash.''

Lyn smiled, shaking her head in wonder. "You know, you drive me crazy sometimes...but I really envy you. You always have everything under control, nothing ever goes wrong when you're in charge. I guess you're the most together person I've ever met.''

An odd expression crossed his face, like surprise, or even denial. "Is that what you think?''

"Don't you?''

It was strange. Until now, if anyone had asked him that question his answer would have been an unqualified yes. He liked his life. He had spent years working and building to get everything the way he liked it. His days were full and his nights were peaceful, and until he had met Lyn he thought he had everything he wanted. But now . . . something had changed. He wasn't so sure what he wanted anymore.

He looked at her for another moment, then turned his eyes to the menu. His tone was negligent, but it seemed to hide a deeper emotion. "I'm almost thirty years old; I share my meals with a dog and my bed with three cats. Does that sound like a man who's got his life together to you?"

Now Lyn was surprised, and cautiously intrigued. "I thought you liked it that way."

He raised his eyes to her again. They were frank, and unapologetic, and as deep as the sea that whispered around them. "It's the way things are," he said simply. "And the way I am. Not the best of all possible worlds, but the best I can do."

"What would you change?" she asked curiously.

But a spark came into his eyes, and the moment of seriousness was gone. "My sleeping companions?" he suggested.

Lyn lifted an eyebrow in amused reproval, but she chose not to reply to that.

If Lyn could have ordered a fantasy evening, it would have been precise in every detail to the one she shared with Casey. The warm breeze that tickled the curls around her face and caused the candles to dance within their crystal globes; the sighing rush of the sea as the indigo tide swept in, closer and closer, until it licked the pilings beneath her feet . . . and Casey, strong and bronzed, sitting across from her, the breeze occasionally tugging at his hair, his eyes crinkling with a smile, moonlight and candlelight turning his eyes to rich velvet.

The meal was a sensual orgy in itself, the vegetables so sweet and tender they could have been plucked only minutes before they reached the kitchen, flaky grouper in an exquisite pecan sauce, a white wine so delicate it barely whispered across the tongue... And there was Casey. The curve of his long fingers as he lifted his wineglass fascinated her, the sound of his voice or his low chuckle vibrated through her body with chords of pleasure. Her eyes kept returning to his throat, and the dip of his collarbone as revealed by the open button of his shirt, and she thought how handsome he was, and how lucky she was to be with him, and how different her life had become in the short time she'd known him.

The moon, when it rose, was as perfect as an oil painting, reflecting shimmering ripples off the ocean from horizon to tide line, and Lyn sat sipping her coffee, enchanted by the effect. "I don't know whether that was the most delicious meal I've ever tasted," she said, "or whether it only seemed that way because I'm having such a good time."

His smile was like a mirror of her own contentment. "I hope it's a little of both. Would you like to take a walk?"

She closed her eyes and breathed in the sea air scented with candle wax and gourmet aromas. "No," she sighed. "Yes. I want to stay here forever. And I want to walk on the beach all night. Oh, Casey, what a wonderful evening. Thank you."

He reached across the table and took her hand. "If I had known it would make you this happy, I would have thought of it sooner." He squeezed her fingers briefly, tenderly. "Come on. Let's walk."

They skirted the restaurant and walked down onto the beach, staying on the firm sand where the cold water did not reach. They laughed as Rabbit, released from his leash, investigated the lapping tide cautiously, then yelped and ran back to them when the cold water hit his nose. Casey held her hand. Lyn thought she couldn't ask for more.

"Do you know," Casey said after a time, "you might not believe this, but sometimes I think I work too hard. I forget how to relax."

Lyn chuckled. "You're right, I don't believe it."

His grin filtered down to her through the moon-drenched night. "Are you saying I'm a hard taskmaster?"

"Harder on yourself, I think," Lyn replied, "than on anyone else."

"You're probably right," he agreed after a moment. "I never thought about it that way."

"I guess expecting too much from yourself is one of the prices you pay for being perfect."

"Am I perfect?"

"Ask Rabbit."

Casey reached down and petted the dog who was pressed close to his knee, keeping a wary eye on the water. "He's just a dumb dog, what does he know? Here, Rabbit, get out of here. Go play." He picked up a piece of driftwood and tossed it; after a moment of uncertainty, Rabbit ventured forward after it.

Casey slipped his arm around Lyn's waist and drew her next to him with a grin. "At last, privacy."

She laughed and leaned her head against his shoulder. The sea breeze blew the folds of her gauze skirt against her legs as she walked, moonlight turned the sand to silver, Casey's body was an oasis of warmth and strength against hers. She felt feminine, beautiful . . . and in love.

She wasn't, of course. She couldn't be in love with this man. She couldn't be in love with anyone, but most

especially not with Casey Carmichael, who was everything she didn't need in her life, who was disruptive and
demanding and autocratic, who made her angry and left
her frustrated and made her think far too much. No, she
couldn't be in love with him . . . but it was oh, so nice to
feel as though she were.

With a sudden rush of heady delight, she slid her arm
around his waist in an impulsive embrace. In a smooth
dance of motion, Casey turned her into his arms and
kissed her.

His kiss was as sweet as spring water, as gently infu-
sive as drenching moonlight. She opened her mouth beneath his and let him melt into her, his breath flowing
through her, his heat swelling in her veins and traveling
sluggishly through her limbs with the tingling, life-giving
power of a potent drug. She ached for him, body and
soul. She needed him, as surely as she needed air to
breathe and earth beneath her feet. And then he moved
away.

Casey could not believe he was doing that. He wanted
her so badly he could feel the tremors deep in his muscles, he could hardly think about anything except how
badly he wanted her...but he was pushing her away. How
simple it had all seemed this afternoon, when he asked
her to spend the weekend with him. The only logical solution to the consuming need he felt for her: fulfill that
need and it would go away.

But she was a person, separate and distinct, with needs
even more important than his own. He couldn't ignore
that. And even though he surprised himself by doing so,
he had to make certain she knew where this was leading,
and what she was getting into if it went further.

And maybe he needed a moment to be sure, himself.

He held her face gently between his hands; the unsteady stream of his breath fanned across her heated cheeks. His eyes were alive with passion and dark with intensity. He said softly, "Lyn, think of what you're doing."

Yes, she should think. This was not what she wanted. She could not get involved with him, she could not fall in love with him...and she could not make love to him without doing both. She had made so many mistakes lately; she could not add this to the list. She couldn't afford to hurt herself, or anyone else, anymore.

She lowered her eyes, avoiding the penetrating, soul-stripping lights of his. She said hoarsely, "We'd better start back."

He hesitated, then dropped his hands to her shoulders, massaging the suddenly tense muscles there briefly. Then he said, "No. Not yet."

He took her hand, and led her toward the low jetty a few feet away. She did not protest when he placed his hands on her waist and lifted her up, seating her on the planks. He stood in the sand beside her, not touching her, looking up at her. He said, "Tell me about Philadelphia."

Philadelphia. Where a job, a semifurnished apartment, and a life still waited for her. Where everything she had run away from was shrouded under dust covers and packed away in cardboard file boxes; not buried but in limbo. She couldn't pretend it didn't exist anymore. She couldn't just close her eyes and hope it would go away. Everything that was important to her was back there, and she was here, hiding. That was the problem.

She began to speak lowly, and she would not meet his eyes. At first she kept her voice as matter-of-fact as possible, but her hands were clenched tightly in her lap. She said, "I told you. I did a stupid thing. I was so sure I could set the world on fire, I was always right . . . but this time I was wrong. Very, very wrong."

She took a breath, stiffening her shoulders. "I had only been in Protective Services a few months, and the case records I saw were appalling. You have to understand, that's a high-stress division, mostly child abuse and neglect, and people burn out pretty fast. The caseworkers were . . . well, hard. Almost disinterested. I saw something had to be done, and I thought I was the one who could do it better. So when I got my first case I was really gung ho. We were called in to investigate a child abuse case and . . ." With a great effort, she unclenched her hands. "It's a complicated story, but the mother kept pleading with me not to take the children away and the father seemed to be making a good start toward turning his life around so . . . in the end I recommended to the court that the children be returned to the home. No," she added forcefully. "I *insisted*. I was do damn sure I had the situation under control, that I was right . . ."

Casey's hand rested lightly on her knee, calming, reassuring. Until that moment she had not realized that her muscles were trembling with fine, almost imperceptible quivers, throughout her body. She took another breath and tried to keep her voice even.

"Anyway, on a follow-up visit a few days later . . . the father had a shotgun." Her voice tightened; she couldn't help it. "He dragged me inside and tied my hands with a telephone cord and made me sit on the floor. The mother had run out on the family, God knows where. And the children . . ." Here her voice caught on an indrawn breath. "He had locked them in a closet. I could hear them, crying and screaming, but the worst was when I couldn't hear them at all. The oldest one was only four."

A cool film of perspiration broke out on her body and she was back there, hearing the sounds, smelling the smells, choking on fear... "I—I kept thinking they would smother, or dehydrate, then I thought what it must be like locked in the dark and hearing their father threaten to kill them, to kill us all. Every once in a while he would fire the gun, blasting holes in the ceiling and the walls, and they would start screaming again...." She fought the tremors that threatened to rack her body, fought to keep her breathing even, fought off the nightmare that came back to her in wave after terrifying wave.

"And I couldn't do *anything*. I was so scared. Scared he was going to kill me, or the kids, or himself, scared that it would never be over... Six hours. He held us hostage for six hours. And when the police finally got him to come out... He opened fire on them, and they—they shot him. Killed him."

Then she couldn't fight any longer. The shudders broke through, and the sobs, dry and almost soundless, desperate little gasps for breath. Casey's arms were around her, shielding her, giving her strength, letting her relive what she had to and struggle with what she had to, and holding her until the terror had spun itself out.

The silence was long and dark, and the ocean in the background sounded like whispering voices of accusation. Her face rested against Casey's shoulder, and his arms were warm around her. Her voice sounded strained when she spoke again, barely audible above the murmur of the ocean. "I keep thinking... if I had acted differently, if I had been more careful, more in control. If I hadn't been so damn determined that I could change the world..."

But she didn't finish. Long ago she had learned that what-ifs made no difference; none of it mattered now.

She stepped back and looked at Casey bleakly, trying to force a smile. "So. Now you know my story. I don't deal well with failure, so I came here to escape. Not very brave, not very gallant, not very noble. But that's me, the way I am."

He touched her shoulder in a tender, soothing gesture, and let his hand trail down her arm until his fingers entwined with hers. "You didn't do anything wrong, Lyn," he said. "Nobody can set the world on fire. Sometimes the best we can do is try to light a single candle. You tried, and you have nothing to be ashamed of."

She leaned forward, dropping her head until it rested on his shoulder. She felt weak, drained, yet strangely light inside. Free. It was true, as Casey must have always known, that a burden shared was a burden diminished. He had waited, with patience and insight, until she was ready to talk, knowing that the telling would take away the terror. That was his gift to her.

"Oh, Casey," she whispered, "you were right. You are the best thing that could have happened to me."

He lifted her face, and the look in his eyes was uncertain, disturbed, as though he wanted to say something but did not know how. It unsettled her. Then he smiled, and kissed her lips gently. "I hope so," he said.

The drive home was mostly silent, but it was a gentle quiet, compassionate and unrestrained. It was as though the closeness that had developed between them over the space of the evening left no room for words, elevating their relationship to a new level that each felt compelled to explore within themselves. Lyn rested her head against Casey's shoulder and closed her eyes, not really dozing, but examining the sense of rightness and contentment she felt with cautious wonder, like a fragile treasure she was afraid to grasp too tightly for fear it would break. She felt secure in his nearness. Lying against him drifting on the edge of sleep, feeling his warmth around her and the flex of his muscles against her cheek as he moved his arm, she knew that she wanted it to last for more than an hour.

Lyn turned on a single lamp as Casey walked her inside. It was almost midnight and the neighborhood was quiet; the lamplight cast gentle bluish shadows over the family room and left the rest of the house still and sleepy. Rabbit jumped up on the sofa, yawned loudly, and closed his eyes.

Casey smiled. "It's late," he said, "and you're tired." He touched her cheek with his forefinger, guiding her face to his, and kissed her softly. "Good night, Lyn."

He turned to the door, and opened it. Lyn's heart was beating hard as she watched him. And then she said, "Casey... don't go."

He hesitated. She thought he would ignore her, or that he hadn't heard, or that he would pretend to misunderstand. She knew she wouldn't have the courage to ask again.

Then he turned around, and closed the door softly. His eyes were quiet and gently probing, but he did not cross the room toward her. He asked, "Why?"

Her heart was pounding so now that it hurt her throat. She answered, almost steadily, "Does it matter?"

He came over to her, placing his hands lightly upon her waist. Not drawing her close, not embracing, merely touching. He said, "To me it does."

She placed her hands on his forearms, searching his eyes for something she could not even name... knowing only that, when she looked at him, she found it. And she said, "Because... I've been afraid for so long. And you make me feel strong."

He lowered his eyes, and she could not see the expression there. Her heart was straining, bursting, slamming in her chest as his hands left her waist and she thought he would move away. But instead his hands came to her hair, tugging at the combs that held it away from her face. One by one he loosened the combs and let them drop to the floor. He threaded his fingers through her hair, combing the curls over her shoulders, holding them to the light. His eyes were soft with wonder at the effect. And then he looked at her face, cupping one palm against her cheek. He said huskily, "Let's go into the bedroom."

She did not turn on the light in the bedroom, and the only illumination was the misty flow of moonlight through the louvered shutters. Casey closed the door softly behind them and it wasn't until she heard the muffled snap of the latch that the reality of what was about to happen leaped through her nerves with a jolt. In a moment she would be naked with this man, his body wrapped around hers, vulnerable to him, open to him. There would be no more hiding, no more uncertainty. Nothing would be the same after that.

She turned to him. Her throat was dry, her stomach tight with anticipation. She could feel her pulse fluttering like sparrow's wings against the back of her throat.

He slipped his hands beneath her hair, caressing the back of her neck. His warmth flowed through her, heightening the nerve endings along her spine, spreading a flush across her skin. Without moving an inch, her body seemed to expand and yearn toward him.

The rich deep light in his eyes held her as he said softly, "You make my head spin. I can't think straight."

"I've never been able to think when I'm with you."

"I wish I could resist you. Something tells me you are very dangerous."

"I don't want to be," she whispered. "I just want to be loved . . . tonight, by you."

"Tonight," he said on a breath, "you are adored by me."

His fingers whispered along the curve of her collarbone, following the sweeping neckline of her dress. He took the first small button and unfastened it, and the second.

There were twenty-two buttons, and Lyn counted every one with a catch of her breath, a new, startled leap of her pulses. When she lifted shaking fingers to help him he gently brushed them aside, releasing the buttons one by one, inch by fraction of an inch. His fingers brushed against her breasts, trailed along her sternum, feathered across her waist and her abdomen until the buttons ended in a narrow point just below her navel. He lifted his hands and pushed the material off her shoulders, tugging the sleeves over her hands, and the gauzy garment fluttered to the floor around her feet. Slowly he slid the straps of her slip off her shoulders and down her arms, his eyes followed the drifting fabric as it exposed her breasts, the length of her rib cage, the slim indentation of her waist, until she stood before him clad in nothing but her panties.

She was trembling as he hooked his fingers into the scrap of material and gently tugged them over her hips. He knelt to lift her feet, one by one, to free her of the garment. His hands drifted upward along her legs as he straightened, caressing the shape of her calves and her knees, and the long line of her thighs. When his hand slipped between her legs and cupped that most sensitive part of her she felt a flare of dizziness that left her weak; she clutched his shoulders and gasped his name.

He pulled her into his embrace, his mouth covering hers. She felt the hardness of his body through his clothes, his muscles straining. She tasted the heat of his neck and the roughness of his jaw as her hands tangled in his hair and then pushed impatiently at his jacket, fumbling with the buttons of his shirt. His shirt was open and his bare chest pressed against her, flesh against flesh, flame fanning fire.

They lay together on the bed, their clothes discarded, as a medley of sensations seared Lyn's consciousness and blazed away, only to be replaced by more vivid, demanding impressions. The shape of his back and shoulders beneath her exploratory fingers, the texture of his skin, smooth and damp and hot. His calves, twining around hers, the softly furred strength of his thighs, the sharp bones of his ankles. His taste, his warm, rich scent, and the ache that wound inside her and threatened to explode.

His thighs gently nudged hers apart and his hand slipped beneath her neck, lifting her face to his as he sank into her. She wrapped her arms around him and she opened her mouth to him, drinking of him, consumed by him, filled with him. Slow, drawing rhythms that left her empty and then pressed into the core of her, tightening the need, expanding the pleasure, stretching the sensation to its thinnest point. She was endlessly, wholly enveloped in him, in what they were together, in what he made her feel. Life, as intensely as she had ever known it, was what he gave her. He made her feel new, filled with power and the certainty of need. With him, anything was possible. And when the last convulsive waves of pleasure exploded around them and they clung to each other, drained and drifting in wonder, the only thing she knew was that this was right. If everything else in her life had been wrong, this night with Casey was right, and she only wondered how she could have failed to know it for so long.

She lay with her face against his heartbeat, her arm stretched across his body and her fingers entwined with his. She could feel his breathing, and the gentle tugging motions his fingers made in his hair.

He said, "I used to lie awake at night, imagining what it would feel like to have your hair tangled across my throat like this."

She turned her face a little to look at him. "You never told me."

A slight hesitance. "No. I never did."

"And? Does it feel like you imagined?"

"Better." His voice was low and drowsy, a rich vibration that seemed to go through her soul. "It feels . . . too good to be true." His fingers tightened on hers. "Ah, Lyn, I wish . . ."

"What?"

But he didn't finish. Instead he brought her fingers to his lips and kissed them tenderly.

"Casey," she whispered, and lay her face against his heart again. "I'm falling in love with you."

She felt his deep inhalation of breath, and the brush of his lips across her hair. "I know," he said softly. And he lay back against the pillows. "God help me, I know."

Eight

Atop the plaster of Paris boulder the cougar crouched, twitched its tail and prepared to spring. On the ground below the man rolled over and fumbled for his gun. The cougar roared and launched itself into the air.

Casey shouted, "Sheba, cut!"

Sheba landed gracefully on the ground and began to lick her fur. Casey walked up to her, snapped on her collar and chain, and gave her a treat from his pocket.

The same sequence had been repeated six times so far today, but this time the director announced, "Okay, great. Perfect. Let's get a shot of the dead cat and then we can wrap it up for today. Makeup, get some blood over here. Casey, you need any help?"

Casey waved and replied, "I've got it under control." The director, as well as the makeup staff, looked immensely relieved.

Casey grinned as Lyn came over to him. "I wonder what he'd do if I said yes?"

Lyn returned his grin and cautiously stroked Sheba's head. "Hire you an assistant, probably."

"I've already got one." Casey ran a brief affectionate hand along her back and for the moment that their eyes met the crowded set disappeared, the clamor of voices and equipment receded to the background, and there was only the two of them. Then the makeup girl appeared with a canister of fake blood and Casey turned his attention to her as she explained, somewhat nervously, how to apply it.

Sometimes it worried Lyn, how much she had begun to depend on those secret moments, those shared looks, over the past week. The days were a blur, lost in the euphoria of newfound passion, punctuated by the memory of Casey's touch, the smile in his eyes, the nights spent wrapped in his arms. They worked together, they played together, and there had been no question of her coming with him to Orlando for the shoot. To be apart from him, even for a few days, would be an unbearable jolt to the rhythms of her life.

Yet there was an uneasiness within Lyn that she could not define, a restlessness that haunted the back of her mind. Though life had never been more beautiful, she sometimes felt as though she were still in limbo, passing time, waiting. And she did not know what she was waiting for.

Casey handed Sheba's leash to Lyn as he began applying the artificial gore to Sheba's shoulder and neck. "Hold her still, honey, don't let her lick it off. This is why I vote against realism in the movies. This stuff is going to be a mess to clean up."

Lyn smiled ruefully as she tightened the chain and reached into her own pocket for a liver-flavored treat. "Who would've thought a month ago that I'd be holding this cougar and feeding it out of my hand?"

Casey's eyes sparked as he glanced up at her. "You've changed," he agreed.

And perhaps that was it, Lyn realized slowly. She was changing, growing out of the cocoon of fear and uncertainty that had brought her here, feeling things she had never allowed herself to feel before and becoming stronger every day. Because of Casey, she was different in a thousand subtle ways. And because of Casey, she needed more than she ever had in her life.

Casey must have noticed an alteration in her expression, because he said, "So, how do you like the big-time movie scene? Not quite as glamorous as the magazines picture it, is it?"

"Oh, I don't know." She smiled. "Glamour is in the eye of the beholder, I guess. And I'm glad I came." She paused to blot her forehead with the back of her hand. "It's hard work, though, isn't it? And hot."

"You think this is something, wait until July."

Though he didn't stop his work to look up at her, the last part of the sentence seemed to be cut a little short, and Lyn could see his shoulders tense. She felt the tension seep into her own body as if by osmosis. July. Neither of them knew whether she would be here in July, and the future was one thing they avoided talking about with an almost deliberate resolve.

The future was a hazy fog on a distant horizon, and lurking within it were decisions, promises, resolutions, changes. None of it had anything to do with today, with Casey and her and the tenuous magic in which they enshrouded themselves. There were questions that needed to be answered, choices that needed to be made, and out of them a future would grow. Until then, they both would continue to live in limbo.

And Lyn felt again that haunting sense of uneasiness, of something not quite right. It was nothing more than a future that, sooner or later, would have to be faced.

But, apparently, it was not to be today.

Sheba, sensing her mood, began to fidget restlessly, and when Lyn tightened the leash Sheba snarled. Casey stood up, wiping his hands on a towel, and took the leash. "You look hot, and tired. There's not much more to do here, why don't I just meet you back at the hotel?"

"Are you sure?"

"It won't take me more than an hour."

She hesitated, but the thought of a nice, tepid shower, something cool to drink from room service, and a fluffy hotel robe compelled her. She said, "Well, okay. I need to call home and check the answering machine anyway. Pat will kill me if I let any jobs get away."

His lips brushed hers with a kiss, and his eyes sparked another one of those endless moments charged with promise. "An hour," he repeated.

The warmth of his touch lingered with her all the way back to the hotel. There was something nice about waiting for him. Something wonderful in knowing that, even in a strange hotel room in an unfamiliar city, she wasn't alone. There was always another part of her out there somewhere, waiting for her, just as she was waiting for him.

She showered, tousling her hair with her fingers and letting it air-dry in curls around her face as she changed into fresh shorts and a T-shirt. She did not have to wonder whether Casey would want to go out tonight; he would be tired, just as she was, and they'd order room service. She smiled as she realized how well she was learning to read him, and wondered where the old saying, "familiarity breeds contempt" had ever come from. The more she knew of Casey, the more she liked . . . or perhaps that was just because she was in love. And even she was wise enough to know that that grand euphoria did not last forever.

She sat on the bed to dial Pat's home number. She didn't really expect anything important, but Pat might have called, and if any clients had left messages, Lyn would have to return their calls from here, before they found another sitter.

There was one message on the machine. It was from Lois Waters, Lyn's supervisor in Philadelphia. Lois said simply, "Call me back as soon as you get a chance. It's important, and I think we should talk about this."

Every muscle in Lyn's body tensed with dread. Memories as dark as winter alleyways crept through her, a stark and unwelcome contrast to the Florida sunshine that danced on the carpet. She did not want to return that call. She didn't want to be connected, by thought or deed, to the nightmare she had left behind. And another Lyn, the Lyn who, beaten and bruised, had sought shelter in her sister's home almost a month ago, would have ignored the message. She would have hung up the phone and felt not even a tug of guilt as she wandered away to take a nap or bask in the sun.

Lyn glanced at the door. If only Casey would come back now, distract her, give her an excuse not to call. She could put it off until tomorrow, maybe she'd forget. But Casey wasn't even due for another half hour, and she couldn't put it off forever. Squaring her shoulders, she dialed the Philadelphia telephone number.

Lois was in, and took her call immediately. She had never been one to waste words on the amenities, and she got right to the point.

"How much longer do you need, Lyn? This is beginning to look like less of a leave of absence than a sabbatical. We can't hold this position open forever."

Some of the tension seeped from Lyn's body as she realized the subject of the call was not going to be as dramatic as she feared. "I understand, and I never meant for you to be left shorthanded. I told you, if you need to fill the position—"

"Already done," Lois said crisply. "There are people out there dying on the streets, young lady, and they don't have time to wait for you to make up your mind."

The announcement struck Lyn with a jolt that surprised her. She should have been relieved; the decision about whether or not to return to the life she'd left behind had been made for her. The position had been filled; she had no job. But instead of relief, she felt a stab of hurt, and jealousy. Of loss. She had been replaced, and until that moment she had not realized that she was not at all ready to let go.

She said, trying to force lightness into her tone, "I thought you said this was important."

"It is. As you very well know, there are dozens of eager-eyed young things lined up and ready to take over the job you left behind. I never expected you to come back to that. But I need to know what you're going to do, and I need to know soon. There's an opening in administration, and I've already recommended you for the position."

For a moment Lyn could not speak.

Lois went on, "It's where you belong, Lyn, you and I both know it. Making policy, making the decisions, making a difference. You've rotated through every department in the service and you've got the experience for it. God knows there's no one more qualified. But more importantly, there aren't too many people left who still have the vision you do, and *that's* what we need. So what do you say?''

"I..." Lyn cleared her throat. Her mind was racing and she tried to focus on something, to concentrate. What she ended up focusing on was the picture of a cartoon duck on the wall. "You've caught me off guard," she confessed. "I hadn't really thought..."

"What's there to think about?" Lois demanded. "You've spent your whole career preparing for this. Now I know it's not the most glamorous job in the world and the pay isn't going to keep you in a new German-made coupe every year, but that's not what you got into social services for, is it?''

Lyn threaded her fingers through her hair, pushing back the damp curls. Her voice was soft, and more uncertain than she expected it to be as she replied, "I'm not sure I know why I got into social services anymore."

There was a brief silence. Then Lois said quietly, "I'll tell you why. Because you wanted to do something important. To make a small difference in a big way, to change lives. Well, here's your chance. Lyn..." For the first time since Lyn had known her, Lois's voice was actually gentle. "I know what happened to you was rough. And combat fatigue gets to all of us. But coming out of something like that all the stronger for it is what makes the difference between living and just surviving. You've got what it takes, Lyn. I've always known that, even if you've had your doubts. And we need you back."

Lyn hung up the phone feeling dazed and disturbed...and excited, disoriented, disbelieving. This was the chance of a lifetime. The opportunity to do something important, something she believed in, to make a difference in a monumental way. She could *do* this. She had spent years working for it, she was ready, she was qualified. And she wasn't afraid.

Because of Casey, she wasn't afraid anymore.

Because of Casey, she was ready to go back. And to start living again would mean leaving him behind.

There was a hollowness in her stomach, and something very nearly akin to guilt leaped to her throat when she heard the turn of the key in the lock. Casey came in, his step easy and his hair sun tousled, bringing light into the room with no more than his presence. She realized that whenever she thought of paradise, she would think in terms of him...the green of his eyes, the gold of his hair, the warm sand color of his skin.

"I brought you a present," he announced, and produced from behind his back a hat shaped like a pair of mouse ears.

She laughed as he settled the cap on her head. "Wait a minute, I'm not sure I like the implication. Does this mean I remind you of a mouse?"

"No," he said, and the sparkle in his eyes gentled as he caught a handful of curls on either side of her face and crumpled them playfully. "It means that whenever I think of fantasyland, I think of you. Being with you is like being on vacation all the time and..." His smile faded as he leaned forward, touching her lips lightly with his own. "A man could get very used to that, very quickly."

There was a catch in her throat as she lifted her arms to encircle him, needing suddenly to be held, to drown out the conflicting needs and emotions inside her with the simple certainty of his strength. But he caught her wrists lightly, and kissed her nose. "Let me get a shower, I'm filthy and covered with cat hair. Do you want to have room service tonight?"

She smiled as she watched him go into the bathroom. "Sounds great."

She opened the door to the balcony and stepped outside, leaning against the rail. The back of the hotel overlooked a distant highway and a swampy tangle of trees and vines, shadowed in twilight and the last orange rays of the sun. The faraway sound of traffic was hypnotic, the spray of the shower from inside the room soothing. She thought, *How can I leave this place? How can I go back to two feet of snow and mud-splattered boots and under-heated tenement rooms? Why would anyone in her right mind want to?*

How could she leave Casey, who, in a few short weeks, had brought her more happiness than she had ever known?

But the trouble with fantasyland was that, sooner or later, the illusion wore thin, and no one could stay on vacation forever.

Casey came out, wearing a white hotel robe that barely skimmed his knees, and nothing else. His hair was damp, his face clean-shaven and smooth. He stood behind her, slipping his arms around her waist, and the scent of spicy soap and shaving lotion drifted over her.

She leaned back against him, resting her shoulders against his chest, her thighs against his. Neither of them spoke for a long time, and measure by measure the tension and uncertainty within Lyn drifted away, drawn into his strength. Nothing seemed insurmountable with Casey, no problem was overwhelming when he was around. It was hard to concentrate on all that was wrong, and easy to just let go and revel in how right everything felt.

But it wasn't really right. She knew that. And sooner or later decisions had to be made.

It was almost as though he was following the course of her thoughts, or perhaps in their closeness, her mood was simply absorbed by him. He said quietly, "You know, it would be really easy to get attached to you. That scares me a little."

She didn't move, or turn her head to look at him, but everything within her was abruptly suspended in alertness, waiting. "Why?" she whispered. "Why does it frighten you?"

For a moment he didn't answer, but she could feel a slight tightening of his arms around her waist. "A long time ago," he answered at last, "I learned that nothing in life really belongs to me. I can borrow the good things for a while, and then it's time to let go. You're one of the good things, Lyn. Maybe the best. But you don't belong to me."

Lyn understood, too painfully, too well. Everyone he had loved he had lost. He was afraid, just as she had been when she first came here, and he was hiding, just as she had been. Yet he had been the one who taught her it was all right to care, he had been the one who had shown her the importance of becoming involved with life again. How could she give back to him what he had given to her? How could she make him see that loving did not always mean losing?

Because suddenly it was very clear, very simple. She did not want to leave Casey; she *couldn't* leave him. Before Casey, there had been no reason to get up in the morning, days were only filled with automatic motions, nights were endless and she was hollow inside. He had given her purpose, clarity, meaning. With Casey there was life; without him, only emptiness.

It was so simple. She belonged here, with him. There was no choice. She felt weightless with relief.

She said, "I do belong to you, Casey. Remember—you save a person's life and you're responsible for her forever?"

She thought she heard the hint of a smile in his voice. "That only applies to dogs. Besides, I didn't save your life."

"Yes, you did," she whispered, and closed her eyes. "Oh, yes you did."

He rested his chin atop her head, then turned his cheek to the texture of her chair. She could feel the deep expansion of his chest with his breath. "You feel so right in my arms, Lyn."

She said, "Casey, I want to tell you—"

But he did not want to hear what she had to say. He did not want to hear anything else that would pull at his heart, the way her last words had done, or make him want more than he could possibly have...the way almost everything she said did. So he pressed his lips against her neck and he whispered, "Let's make love."

He felt her relax against him, sink into him. "Don't you know?" she answered softly. "We are. Whenever we're together...we are."

And that was just it. Being with her, everything about her, was like a symphony of love, of chords that meshed and melodies that lingered. It took him from the heights of ecstasy to the depths of pathos, echoing through the chamber of his soul with longing...too perfect, too beautiful, to ever be his. Being with her was a constant tug of war with his emotions, pulling him toward her while he tried to hold himself back, desperately fighting to maintain control. And when he felt himself losing the battle, the easiest thing to do was to let himself go, to drown in the physical experience of making love to her, to blot out the dangerous questions, the aching need, with the simple, overwhelming magic their bodies created together.

His hands moved upward, lightly cupping her breasts through the fabric of the T-shirt. Lyn's flesh seemed to swell with slow, heavy pleasure into the warmth of his touch, the whisper of his fingers brushing across the material, defining her shape with feather-soft strokes. She sank into him, letting her pliant muscles take on the shape of his supporting body, his pelvis cradling her buttocks, her spine curving into his torso.

Her breath stopped as his hands moved down and unfastened the top button of her shorts, then the second, and the third. All sensation, all awareness, was concentrated on the slow thin line his fingertips traced down the center of her abdomen, from her navel to the elastic band of her low bikini panties, and then up again. Her flesh tightened, there was an ache between her thighs, and her very womb seemed to contract with anticipation and need.

"Casey," she whispered.

He turned her into his arms, pulling her inside the room. His face was flushed, his eyes were dark with intensity as they moved over her, drinking in every detail. "Sometimes," he said huskily, "I'm almost afraid to touch you, you are so fragile . . . and so precious."

Lyn tugged at the belt of his robe and pushed the material aside with unsteady fingers. She brought her lips to his chest, tasting him, feeling his sharp intake of breath as her tongue traced the outline of his flat brown nipple. Her hands caressed his back, and the smooth flow of his waist, the lean muscles of his thighs. Every part of him she knew by touch alone, and every time she touched him it was as though for the first time. He did belong to her, and she to him. Nothing could ever change that.

They lay together on the bed with arms and legs and fingers entwined. Time took on a new meaning, sunset lingered, and each breath was an eternity unto itself as they fitted themselves together. Casey's eyes were a mirror of lights and dark, reflecting the surge and leap of emotions that went through Lyn as he entered her, filling her with slow, exquisite care, drawing out the moment with agonizing sweetness. Lyn's fingers tightened on his until they ached and she felt the returned pressure of his as his lips brushed over her face, caressing her, drinking of her with light butterfly strokes of his tongue and whispered breaths of half-formed words. Their movements were slow and deep, a luxurious bonding that went beyond passion and touched its source, a merging of souls.

And when at last they lay wrapped tightly in each other's arms the day was gone, and the stillness that enfolded them was like a cradle. Casey said nothing, and neither did Lyn. For the moment their minds, and their hearts, were at peace. Safe in each other's arms, they drifted to sleep.

Lyn was trapped inside a small room, and it was hot. Hot and filthy, smelling of an overflowing garbage pail and the sweat of human fear. A single unshielded bulb dangled from the ceiling and the glare hurt her eyes. There was crying in the background, children crying, and the sound hurt her ears. She wanted to run away from the sound, from the harsh light of the overhead bulb, from the terror that smothered her breath and thundered in her chest, but she couldn't move. As hard as she tried, she couldn't move.

The shadow of a man was silhouetted in the center of the room, larger than life, enormous, stretching from ceiling to floor, looming over her. He was the danger. He held her destiny in his hands. He controlled her every move, her every thought, and if she tried to get away, he would know...

The shadow moved, turned toward her, started to close in on her. Step by step it drew closer and she tried to make herself smaller, tried to scream, tried to run. But she was paralyzed, helpless, he moved closer and closer and there was *nothing she could do*...

He was almost upon her now, and she knew suddenly, desperately, that she must not see his face. She tried to turn her head, tried to close her eyes, but then the light fell upon him and she screamed. It was Casey.

She awoke with a cry, flinging out her hand as she sat upright in bed. She was shaking, clammy with cold perspiration, and disoriented.

Casey sat behind her, holding her shoulders. "Hush," he said softly. "It's okay now. Bad dream?"

A shiver racked her body, and she gulped for breath. After a moment she managed to nod. "Yes." She suppressed another shudder. "Yes," she repeated, and took a breath to strengthen her voice. "I'm sorry I woke you."

He squeezed her shoulders affectionately. "That's what you get for going to bed without your supper."

She tried to smile. "I guess."

He turned on the light and Lyn buried her face in a pillow, squeezing her eyes closed again against the glare. The remnants of the nightmare lingered, thick and oily, like a bad taste in the back of her throat. When she felt Casey's light touch on her shoulder she actually jumped.

He smiled, but he could not completely disguise the concern in his eyes. "Put this on," he suggested, handing her a T-shirt. "It's a little chilly in here."

He had pulled on a pair of jeans, the belt and snap unfastened, his feet and chest bare. Lyn slipped the T-shirt over her head and drew the blanket up to her waist. All she wanted to do was lay her face against Casey's strong bare chest, letting his warmth chase away the chill inside her blood. She reached for him. "Come back to bed."

He sat beside her, drawing her close with one arm around her shoulders. "I'm going to order something to eat in a minute," he said. "Let's talk first."

She did not want to talk. She wound her arms around his waist and held him tightly.

"Lyn," he said quietly, "you know there's only one way to get rid of your nightmares, don't you?"

She would not look at him. "It's just a stupid dream. Everyone has them."

He said, "You have to go back, and face what you left behind."

She was already shaking her head. "I don't want to go back."

He moved a little away from her, taking her chin in his hand and making her look at him. There was no smile in his eyes now, none at all. "You have to. You know that."

Lyn pulled away from him, drawing her knees up to her chin, focusing her eyes on the opposite wall. "I talked to my supervisor in Philadelphia today," she said tonelessly. "There was a message on the answering machine at home. She offered me a promotion. No more casework. A real career advancement. A chance . . . to make a difference."

The silence was long and heavy and endless. Every muscle in her body ached to turn and look at him, but she couldn't. She couldn't make herself move.

And then he said, in a voice curiously devoid of emotion, "Well. That's it then, isn't it?"

She whipped her head around to face him. "What do you mean, that's it?"

He stood up and walked to the window. His gait was easy and his voice showed no signs of strain. "Come on, Lyn, we both knew you had to go back sometime. This was just a vacation for you, it was never meant to be permanent."

A pain like a hot wire tightened from her throat to her solar plexus. "And you and me? That wasn't meant to be permanent, either?"

He didn't answer.

She stood up. "Casey?"

He turned around. The expression on his face was kind, and resigned, but she could see he was holding himself very tightly, forcing gentleness into his tone. "Lyn," he said, "I'm a rescuer. That's what I do. I can't help myself, if I see something—or someone—is hurt, or needy, I take them in, and guide them, and when I've taught them all I can I send them out to do what they were meant to do. That's my life, Lyn, and letting go is part of what I do. I can't keep pets."

Her hands tightened at her sides; an awful pressure twisted in her throat, radiating through her muscles. "I never wanted to be your pet," she said lowly, distinctly. "I am not another one of your strays that you can teach a few tricks and send out into the world to make a living. It doesn't work that way for people, Casey. You can't make it work that way with people!"

For the first time, there was a flicker of pain across his face, and he quickly averted his eyes. He said, "Maybe that's my problem. I'm not accustomed to dealing with people."

And then he looked at her. "But you are, Lyn. That's your special talent, and there are people back in Philadelphia who need that talent. Don't tell me you don't know that."

Suddenly she understood. She understood so clearly that the pain of illumination went through her like a knife. He *wanted* her to go. He was relieved that the moment had finally come. Knowing that she was not destined to be a permanent part of his life had made their affair safe for him, and he had never been afraid that she might leave—only that she might stay.

She said stiffly, "You used me."

"No," he answered quietly. "You used me. I knew it, and you knew it, just like we both knew from the very first that you and I had a time limit. Just because we never talked about it doesn't mean it was a secret; we both knew you would be going back someday soon. So all we could do was make the best of what we had."

Before he finished speaking she was shaking her head. Her hands were clenched tightly at her sides. "No," she said. "It sounds just fine when you say it—so noble and mature and *good*. But that's not the point, is it? It's not the point at all! It's because of you that I'm even able to consider going back—because you taught me not to be afraid, because you brought me out of hiding, because you showed me it was all right to care again. But you're just as scared as I was, and you're hiding, too, in your own way. You showed me how to let go, Casey," she insisted desperately, "why can't you learn to do the same thing?"

His eyes shifted away, and she expected him to deny the parallel, or ignore it. Instead he said, "You're right. I guess I understood what was going on in your head so well because I had been there myself. And maybe...maybe it made it easier for me, knowing that you were leaving soon. Knowing that I couldn't lose what I'd never had."

"You don't have to lose me!" she cried. "Casey, you can't keep holding yourself responsible for things you couldn't control—your parents, your grandmother, your fiancée...they didn't die just because you loved them! Being alive means taking risks, getting involved, *caring*. Isn't that what you've been trying to tell me all these weeks?"

Every word she spoke was like a forked knife, clawing and tearing at pieces of his heart. Didn't she know how much he wanted to be different, how close he had come to losing himself in her? And even now, while he was still in control, while he still had a choice, the temptation to beg her to stay was so great he had to clench his jaw to keep the words back. But the point was that he *was* in control. He did have a choice. And so he said, without looking at her, "What's right for you isn't necessarily what's right for me, Lyn. You need to be involved because that's the way you are. I need to be alone because that's the way I am."

Everything he said was so reasonable, so true. How could she hate him so much for it, why did the pain that tore through her feel so much like a betrayal? Yes, she had known. She had watched him work his gentle therapy on her and she had submitted to it willingly. She had known this place was not her home, and a lifetime with Casey Carmichael was not a possibility...hadn't she? She had walked gladly into his arms and she had known, surely she must have known somewhere in the back of her mind, that it would tear her heart open when she had to leave him. When had she begun to imagine that she might never have to leave him?

Her voice was not quite steady as she said, "What if I don't want to go back?"

His smile was sad and unconvincing. "Are you going to tell me that the woman who wanted to save the world is going to turn her back on a second chance? This is your life, Lyn, what you were meant to do. You want to go back."

The worst was that she had no argument for that. There was a part of her that started adrenaline pumping when she thought of the challenge, a part of her with too much to prove that couldn't just turn away from the opportunity. She wasn't afraid anymore; she needed to *show* them she wasn't afraid. Casey knew that. He knew her far, far too well.

But did he also know about the side of her that couldn't exist apart from him? Did he know that when she thought of life without him it felt like winter winds blowing through her soul? Did he care?

She felt tired, drained, defeated by all that battered her. And she answered dully, "I don't think I know what I want to do."

He walked over to her, and touched her arm. But his caress held no magic now; he could have been across the room from her, or across the country. He said, "Let's not talk about it anymore tonight. I'll order some dinner." Then he bent his head, and she could not avoid looking at him. "It'll be all right, Lyn," he said. "Really." But there was nothing in his eyes to convince her, and she couldn't meet his gaze for very long.

There were no more nightmares that night. Lyn lay in bed beside Casey, who was close enough to embrace but as far away as the next planet, and she did not sleep at all. The real nightmare, she was very much afraid, had only begun.

Nine

They arrived at Casey's house around ten the next morning. Looking back, Lyn could not believe that they had passed over twelve hours without talking about anything more significant than the weather. But when she considered her own cowardice, and Casey's natural ability to take control of any situation and manipulate it to his liking, perhaps it was not so surprising after all.

She felt a little dazed, stripped and raw inside, and yet too numb to really feel the pain. Or perhaps it was simply that she had not yet accepted the loss. She refused to believe that there was not some compromise, some middle ground between what she wanted and what she needed. At that time, she still maintained the illusion that she had some control over her life, and she only knew that she could not lose Casey.

She could stay here. She could get a job, an apartment...and start all over as a caseworker investigating child abuse and welfare fraud and late support payments, working long hours for little reward and growing nothing but older. Everything within her recoiled at that. She couldn't go back on the streets again, struggling with futility day after day. At least in Philadelphia there was a chance for her to live up to her potential, to do what she had been trained to do and had dreamed of doing all her life. There was no future for her here, and how could she give up everything when the man who would have made it all worthwhile wouldn't even ask her to stay?

But I don't want to go back. That one sentence kept repeating itself over and over in her head, against all logic, against all that was reasonable and right. *I don't want to go back*. She was a different person here, she had everything she wanted here, life was full of possibilities here. How could she go back to the life she had left behind when the only things that mattered were right here before her eyes?

Casey, she thought. *Don't let me do this. Don't let me make another mistake. . . .*

But Casey's smile was absent as he glanced across the car seat at her, his demeanor unconcerned. As far as he was concerned, the matter was already settled.

When they reached home, Casey went to talk to his kennel boy and check on the animals, and Lyn waited on the front porch. She would have gone inside, made herself something to drink, prolonged the visit. But she didn't want to. She didn't want to wander through the house with its familiar scent of hyacinths and its cozy clutter, to sit at the table where they had shared more than one meal, to gaze upon the bed with its rumpled sheets that were, more likely than not, sprinkled with cat hair, and remember the last time they had made love there. So she stood outside, and waited.

Montana came up the steps, sat down in front of her, and lifted his paw. Lyn bent to shake his paw, stroking his head absently. "Hiya, fella. Since when did you learn manners?"

"He's always had them," Casey said. "He just doesn't see the need to use them much of the time."

He had Rabbit on a lead, and the dog was bouncing and leaping and snapping playfully on the leash. For the first time, Casey didn't bother to correct him, and Rabbit's behavior clearly showed the lack of discipline.

"Here you go," Casey offered the leash to her. "Safe and sound and not much the worse for wear."

Lyn did not take the leash, and after a moment, Casey bent to loop it around the rail post at the bottom of the steps. "What are you going to do with him, anyway, when you go?" he asked casually. "Take him with you?"

Lyn's voice was low and shaky. "Ask me to stay, Casey."

For a moment Casey froze in his movements, his shoulders rigid and his back to her, then he said briefly, "I can't do that."

He straightened and came up the steps to her, perfectly calm, perfectly in control as he always was. "Look, Lyn," he said, "this is not a big deal. I don't see why you're agonizing over it. It's cut-and-dried. You needed some time to get yourself together and you've done it, but now it's time to go back where you belong and get to work."

She set her jaw stubbornly against the pain that was gnawing at her, but she was not going to beg him. *Damn it, Casey, don't do this....* "Maybe I belong here," she said.

Frustration flashed across his face and he made an impatient gesture with his wrist. "Doing what? Emptying kitty litter and walking dogs for the rest of your life? You're better than that, Lyn, you *deserve* better than that! Stop fooling yourself, and stop dragging this out. It's over."

The words hit her like a blow to the chest, but even more final was the look on his face. It was hard, devoid of emotion or warmth, the face of a stranger. *It's over.* His eyes were already looking beyond her and toward his next project.

Her voice sounded choked, lost in the well of pain that was rising inside her as she said, "You don't care, do you? You don't care at all."

His lips tightened, and this time his eyes were turbulent, anger mixed with impatience and too many other things for her to read. "Damn it, Lyn, what do you want me to say? That I care so much that just looking at you now is tearing me apart inside? That I was a fool to get involved with you in the first place when I knew how it would end? That I'm sorry? Well, I am sorry, sorrier than I've ever been in my life and it's killing me, letting you go. What more do you want from me?"

"I want you to fight for us!" she cried. Her eyes were hot with tears and her fingernails dug into her palms. "I want you to stop being so damned perfect and noble and *right* and tell me not to go! I want—I want you to love me!"

His eyes went swiftly from fire to ice. She thought in that moment that everything would be all right, that he would say the words she needed to hear and he needed so badly to say, and she was so certain, so desperately, hopefully certain, that her breath actually stopped in anticipation.

But then his eyes went blank, his jaw hardened. And he said simply, "I can't, Lyn. I'm sorry."

And that was it. She could not make him love her, she could not insist that he needed her. It was over.

An errant breeze stirred leafy shadows across the porch, then was still. A dog bayed from the kennel, and a smaller dog took up the chorus. A bird let out a sudden chittering overhead, and in a moment, its mate answered from the distance. There was movement, there was sunlight, the world went on about its business, unaware. But in that moment all the life drained out of Lyn and left her numb.

She moved past Casey and down the steps. When she reached Rabbit she stopped. Her voice sounded distant and detached, very unlike her own. "Will you take the dog?"

"No." Casey's response was brief, a bit too sharp. "I don't want him."

Lyn fumbled with the leash, and somehow managed to release the loop. "Come on, Rabbit."

Rabbit leaped toward the steps.

"Come on!" She jerked the leash, and Rabbit looked at her curiously, then lunged toward Casey again.

"Rabbit, stop it!" To her horror, Lyn felt the threat of a sob in her throat. She grabbed the leash with both hands and pulled. *"Come on!"*

Rabbit looked at her, and looked at Casey. He dug in his heels and refused to budge.

Then Casey stepped forward, and made a sharp gesture with his hand. "Go!" he commanded harshly.

Rabbit looked up at him, and emitted a single whine. But when Lyn jerked on the leash the next time the dog fell into place beside her, and with only one last look over his shoulder, followed her obediently to the car.

Lyn did not cry. All the way home the tears were blocked up in her chest, a huge dam of pain that strained at the fragile walls of her control, but she couldn't seem to release it. It was almost as though she had forgotten how. Everything seemed distant, unreal, disconnected. Perhaps there were some losses, some shocks, that were too big for tears. Perhaps she was simply afraid that, once she gave way to the agony that was swelling and clawing inside her it would devour her.

Perhaps she thought that she could control it, or ignore it, just as Casey had.

She didn't remember driving home, or getting out her key, or fumbling with the lock. When she opened the door, Pat was there.

"Hi." She stood up casually and tossed the magazine she'd been reading on the sofa, looking as though she had never been gone at all. She didn't appear to notice her sister's haggard face, or the dog that lunged and struggled on the other end of the leash.

"Pat." Somehow, even through the numbness, surprise and confusion penetrated. "What are you doing home?"

Pat gave an airy wave and a smile. "Oh…I got bored. And I missed you. And—"

Her voice broke, and her hand fluttered to her lips to suppress a sob. Without another word, the two sisters stumbled into each other's arms.

Lois gave Lyn two more weeks in which to report to work. Lyn knew she could have better used that time by getting herself reoriented in Philadelphia, settling in, and doing some off time studying and reading before she officially took over her new job, but she stayed in Florida. She told herself that, after all Pat had done for her, she really couldn't run off and leave her when her sister was feeling so down, but the truth was that Pat was handling the unhappy ending to her own love affair with typical stoicism and poise.

"There were just too many problems," Pat told her with a sad little smile when at last she was ready to talk about it. "I mean, I have my house here, and my business—it may not be much, but I love it. A doctor can't just up and move his practice, and...I didn't want to give up what I already had." She lifted her shoulders, and gazed mistily into her glass of iced tea. "He had grown children, an ex-wife and two houses to support. And I had a husband with whom I'm still very much in love. There was just so much excess baggage from the past, for both of us, and it would have been hard to adjust. Maybe it would have been worth it, but it would have been hard. And I think ... as you get older, you're not quite as willing to take a chance on change. It was, I don't know, safer for me just to stay with the status quo."

Lyn thought that was the saddest thing she had ever heard.

Perhaps it was selfish, but comforting her sister made it easier for Lyn to deal with her own pain. It was hard to feel sorry for oneself when someone else needed you ... which was exactly what Casey had tried to teach her when he first insisted that she come to work for him.

But the bad dreams didn't go away, and when she awoke at night gasping and shaking there was no one there to comfort her.

Lyn devoted herself, in the two weeks that remained to her in Florida, to working with Rabbit. She brushed him, she walked him, she bribed him with treats to come when he was called; she took him on pet-sitting jobs and to the bank and to the grocery store, until he became so familiar with the routine that when he saw Lyn pick up her purse he would run to the car and wait to be let into the back seat. She spent every spare moment working with him, thinking up little tricks for him to do and then teaching him, through long hours of patient repetition, to execute the simplest of them. It was a form of therapy—for her, for the dog, and for Pat, who, after the first shocked protests, had not only begun to accept Rabbit's presence in her home, but actually liked him.

Rabbit's favorite game was hide-and-seek. With the command "Find Pat!" the dog would scurry through the house and yard, sniffing the ground, checking closets and behind draperies and under the furniture until he found whatever ingenious hiding place Pat had come up with, and helped himself to the dog biscuit that was invariably in her hand.

After one such exercise Pat commented, "That dog is smarter than most people, you know that? How many more tricks are you going to teach him?"

Lyn shrugged. "He's really not all that smart. He still runs away when you take the leash off and he growls at the postman and cowers in traffic. He's got to do better than that before anybody'll want to adopt him."

"Like what?" Pat insisted incredulously. "Look at him! He brings in the paper and carries packages and finds things that are lost. And that cute thing you taught him where he barks when you whistle . . ."

"I didn't teach him that," Lyn pointed out uncomfortably. "He just does it. He's supposed to *come* when I whistle."

"Well, it's still cute. And I've never seen a happier dog! Anyone would be glad to have him—what more do you want from him?"

Lyn hesitated, watching Rabbit as he slipped a paw between the frame and the screen door, widening the opening, and then squeezed inside, trotting across the tile floor of the family room and settling down to rest in his favorite cool spot. He had put on ten pounds since she had had him, his coat was glossy and his eyes were bright. His ears pricked up whenever he heard his name, and he spent most of his waking hours at Lyn's side, eagerly waiting for the next job to do or the next game to play.

He was a far, far different dog than the one she had found tied to a tree with only a few hours to live, and she had made the difference.

"Casey said it couldn't be done," she murmured.

Pat looked at her, puzzled, "What?"

But Lyn did not respond, a little confused by the newness of what she was thinking. Casey had said Rabbit was untrainable, worthless, and he was the expert. But Casey had been wrong. What else had he been wrong about?

"Besides," Pat added in the most casual of tones, following Rabbit inside, "you don't have to look for anyone to adopt him. He's got a home, right here."

Lyn stared at her. "But—he leaves muddy paw prints on the floor and brings fleas in the house and gets dog hair all over your sofa. You said you didn't want a dog."

Pat shrugged. "I changed my mind. I want this one. And if you're sure you can't take him to Philadelphia with you, then I think he should stay here with me."

Lyn heard herself replying, "I don't think I want to leave him behind."

"Well, I don't think you should, either, but you told me your building doesn't allow dogs, and with the hours you'll be working you won't have much time for him..."

Lyn said abruptly, "I'm going to make some popcorn. You want some?"

She went into the kitchen without waiting for a reply.

For two weeks Lyn had thrown herself into the demands of the moment so completely that she had lost track, not only of the time, but of what she was working toward. She thought she had just been tying up loose ends so she could leave with a clear conscience, but in some ways, without her even being aware of it, she was building a whole new life.

All she had wanted to do was to smooth out some of Rabbit's rough edges so that he would be adoptable; in two short weeks she had done as professional a job with him as Casey could have—perhaps better—without even realizing until this moment that she didn't *want* to put him up for adoption. She had stayed to comfort her sister, to take some of the burden of the business off her while she recovered from her broken heart . . . only Pat's heart wasn't really broken. She had made her own choice of her own free will and, after the first few days, she had not needed Lyn's comfort. It was Lyn who had needed Pat, to make her feel useful, to keep her busy . . . to give her an excuse to stay.

She was supposed to report to the Philadelphia office Monday, and this was Friday. She hadn't even packed her bags yet, and it would be a two-day drive at best. She had been so busy trying to avoid the fact that she would have to leave soon that she hadn't even realized time was running out.

She dreaded going back. Casey didn't want her, Pat didn't need her, and there was no reason for her to stay. There was every reason for her to go. But she had never dreaded anything so much in her life as the thought of the wonderful opportunities that awaited her in Philadelphia.

She brought a bowl of popcorn and two wine coolers into the living room, where Pat was lounging on the sofa, watching the last few minutes of a game show before the evening news came on. Lyn handed her one of the bottled coolers and sat beside her, placing the bowl of popcorn between them.

"What a great supper," Pat said, scooping up a handful of popcorn. "I'm really going to miss you, kid. My diet hasn't taken such a beating since I was seventeen."

"Yeah," agreed Lyn absently, drawing an abstract pattern in the condensation on the wide end of her bottle. "I'm going to miss you, too."

Pat's smile was wistful as she reached across and squeezed Lyn's knee. "I really wish you didn't have to leave. You know, you're the only family I have left and we just don't see each other often enough. I can't tell you how great it's been having you here, even though..." And her face clouded a little. "I didn't get to spend as much time with you as I would have liked."

She tossed a piece of popcorn to an eagerly waiting Rabbit, who snapped it out of the air and swallowed in one movement, then anxiously watched Pat for more. Pat chuckled and tossed him another piece.

"Of course," she added, "I'm happy for you, and so proud of you—at your age, to be offered a job with that kind of responsibility. Chances like that don't come along every day, do they?"

"No," Lyn murmured, sipping from the bottle. "I guess not." Of course, she realized slowly, it really wasn't much of a chance. Taking that job would only be doing what she was trained to do, what she was expected to do, what she had done before.

And then Lyn said, without planning to speak out loud, "But that's not what I want to do."

Pat's hand was arrested in the midst of tossing another piece of popcorn, and she turned to Lyn with surprise stamped on her face. "What?"

"I said," Lyn repeated more clearly, wondering over the words even as she spoke them, "I don't want to take that job. I don't want to go back to Philadelphia."

"But—for heaven's sake, Lyn, I thought you made up your mind! You're supposed to be there Monday. Why in the world did you ever agreed to take it?"

"Because I never had a good reason not to." Lyn's hand tightened on the bottle as the answers came almost more quickly than she could assimilate them; answers to questions she had never bothered to ask herself because if she had she would have never come so close to making the biggest mistake of her life.

"I knew I didn't want to go back from the very first, I kept *telling* him I didn't, but it all happened so fast I never had a chance to think about what I really wanted to do. It was flattering, I guess, and a little exciting, to get the job I'd been working for for so long but I never stopped to think that maybe I wasn't the same person who had wanted that job in the first place!" She turned to her sister, relief coursing through her in waves. "So I said yes because it seemed like the right thing to do, the easy thing to do... because Casey said that was what I should do. But he was wrong," she added softly. "He was *wrong*."

She set the wine cooler down on the coffee table with a thump and glanced at her watch. "I'm calling Philadelphia. Maybe there's still someone in the office."

"Lyn, wait, don't you think you should—"

But Lyn was finished with listening to other people tell her what to do with her life—even her sister, who loved her and wanted her to stay. Lyn was in control now, and she had made the decision.

The familiar theme music of the six o'clock news came on as she was dialing the number, and she knew it was probably too late to reach anyone in the office. She would have to try Lois at home later. She waited impatiently for the connection to be made while Pat watched her anxiously from the sofa.

"Good evening." The television anchorman's handsome face appeared on-screen, his voice sonorous and serious. "The search continues this evening for the last of the three men who were trapped beneath wreckage this afternoon during a construction accident at the Spring Mill mall."

Pat turned around to watch the television. The mall was only a few miles from her house, and in a small town like Summerville, local news was very important. Lyn counted eight rings on Lois's private number with no answer. She racked her brain for another number that might be more likely to be answered.

" . . . And now we go to Jeff Ringer, live at the scene."

"Good heavens," Pat exclaimed involuntarily. "Look at that."

Lyn glanced briefly at the television, her hand poised over the disconnect button as she tried to remember the number of the administration office. An intense young man with a microphone in his hand was standing before the pile of rubble, which had once been a thriving construction site.

"There is good news tonight, as Lincoln Wade, the last of the three men trapped beneath the debris you see behind me, was pulled to safety only seconds ago." The camera flashed to the scene of a stretcher and busy paramedics as the narrative went on. Lyn disconnected and started to dial again, only half her attention on the television set.

"Rescue workers, complete with dogs, have been on the scene since only a few moments after the accident occurred, as you see from this tape shot earlier in the day. The building is so unstable that, at times, efforts were called to a halt for fear for the rescuers' safety."

Lyn stared at the screen, at the dog in the bright red harness and identifying cape picking its way carefully over the broken planks and cement blocks. "Montana!" she whispered.

"And, although all of the trapped men have now been brought to safety, there is one sad note to this story. One of the rescue dogs who worked so remarkably all afternoon to save the trapped and injured construction workers is at this hour buried beneath a portion of a support wall that shifted during the rescue efforts. Although there are no further human casualties, this is indeed an unfortunate ending to a remarkable tale of canine heroism. Back to you in the studio."

"Lyn!" Pat cried, leaping to her feet. "Wait! What are you—"

But Lyn was already out the door.

Ten

Lyn did not even realize that Rabbit had gotten in the car with her until she opened the door and he bounded out beside her. The area in front of the shopping mall disaster was crowded with vehicles and spectators; she pushed her way past fire engines and news vans until she reached the black-and-yellow police tape barrier. And she saw Casey.

He was standing on the other side of the barrier, arguing with a man in shirtsleeves and a hard hat. His khaki shirt was stained with patches of perspiration and dirt, his face was streaked with grime, and his hair had been molded to his head by the hard hat he now held in one hand. His muscles were tense and his gestures were angry and sharp, and though Lyn could not hear his words she could see the intensity blazing in his eyes. The sight of him took her breath away.

Throughout the brief drive to the construction site her heart had been pounding with anxiety and fear, now it all but exploded in her chest. It had been Casey who had been working all day in the midst of this disaster, Casey who had risked his life beneath shattered girders and crumbling walls, Casey who could have been killed and she would never have known about it but for the evening news . . .

She started to push toward him, but a uniformed officer caught her arm. "Sorry, ma'am, you'll have to stay behind the line."

Lyn gestured desperately toward Casey. "I'm with him."

Rabbit barked sharply and dashed under the barrier toward Casey. Casey looked startled when the black-and-white bundle of enthusiasm flung itself against his legs, then his head swung around sharply and his eyes fastened on Lyn's. The sudden surge of joy, of hunger and fierce, desperate welcome that she saw there went through Lyn like an electric current; magnets finding their polarity and coming together with a flash of light and power, across the throng of people and debris-strewn disaster area they found each other, and held.

It might have been the flare of recognition on Casey's face, or it might have been the behavior of the dog, whose companions had certainly distinguished themselves in the eyes of all present today, but after a moment the officer lifted the tape for her. "You'll have to wear this," he said.

Lyn took the hard hat he handed her and scrambled under the barrier.

Casey wanted to run to her, to grab her up and hold her hard and never let her go. He wanted to crush her to him, to cover her mouth with a kiss that was as deep as the agony he had endured these past two weeks, to feel her against him, to smell her, to taste her, to prove to himself that she was really here. She shouldn't have been here. She should have been in Philadelphia. All this time the only thing that had kept his hand away from the telephone was thinking that she was already gone. Now she was here and his heart started beating again, his lungs started drawing air again, for what felt like the first time in two weeks. She was here and his head swam with the impact of her presence. She was running toward him and he wanted to sweep her into his arms...but he stopped himself just in time. He caught her shoulders when she was about two feet away from him, clenching his hands in a fierce grip that was only a reflection of the battle he fought inside, and the words that blazed unspoken between them were so thick they clogged the air.

And then he said hoarsely, "What are you doing here? You're crazy to come here. It's dangerous."

"It's Montana, isn't it?" she demanded urgently.

Casey made himself drop her arms and turned back to the man in the hard hat. *Go away, Lyn,* he thought desperately. *Don't do this to me, not now...* "I'm going in there," he said tightly. "I'm not going to leave that animal to die."

The other man pushed a handkerchief over his sweat-drenched face and said, with obvious difficulty, "Look, Casey, I know how you feel but...the dog is probably already dead. It's not that I don't appreciate everything you've done here today, but I can't let anybody back in here, not until we've secured this place—"

"Then secure it!"

"We're trying! But it's going to take time—"

"I don't have that kind of time!"

Suddenly Rabbit pricked up his ears and barked and, without further warning, started running toward the collapsed building.

"Rabbit! Come back here!" Lyn lunged after him, and then stopped. There was something familiar about the prick of his ears, the enthusiastic swishing of his tail, the purposeful lowering of his head . . . he looked very much the way he did when he was playing hide-and-seek, and was close to finding Pat.

Lyn gripped Casey's arm. "Look!" she exclaimed softly.

Casey's eyes went from the dog, who was squeezing himself between a narrow opening between two pillars, and then back to Lyn. He read the animal's body language and knew what it meant; he just couldn't, for a moment, believe it. Then he placed a firm hand on Lyn's arm, pushing her aside. "Stay here," he commanded.

The other man shouted, "Casey, damn it!" And then, "Hey, lady, you can't—"

Lyn ignored him, just as Casey had. She pulled the hard hat on and ran after Casey, through the shattered remnants of the doorway where Rabbit had gone.

Casey turned angrily when he felt her presence behind her. "What are you doing? I told you to stay put!"

Lyn replied, "I don't take orders from you anymore, Casey Carmichael. Rabbit's my dog and you don't know how he works."

Casey was torn between astonishment, outrage and frustration . . . and need, and joy, because it was Lyn, and she was here. But he couldn't think about that now. He just couldn't. "Works? What the hell are you talking about? Lyn, get out of here before—"

Lyn whistled sharply, and in a moment heard the muffled *ruff* of a reply. She gestured to the left. "He went that way, and we'd better hurry before you lose him again.''

Casey registered momentary confusion, but it was quickly replaced by adamance. "No," he said. "I've worked this building all day, I know how dangerous it is. Now get out of here before you get hurt."

"No."

"For God's sake, Lyn!" He gripped her arm, his face taut with pain and despair. "I'm not going to lose you, too!"

She met his eyes steadily. "Damn right you're not," she said softly. "Now, let's go!"

It was hot inside the building, and the only illumination was the dying daylight that filtered down through cracks and holes. The air was thick with cement dust and plaster, and the occasional creak of yet another failing support beam made them both freeze in place, waiting for the remainder of the building to fall down around them. For most of the time the passage was so narrow that they had to edge along in single file; finally they were forced to crawl.

"You're a liar," Lyn said, keeping her voice low between breaths of exertion, almost afraid that anything louder than a whisper would start a chain reaction that would end in an avalanche.

They were on their bellies in a narrow tunnel that had apparently been carved out of the rubble during the rescue of the construction workers. In places the floor beneath them was chipped concrete, in others it was gravel and earth. Huge pipes and pieces of lumber were balanced precariously overhead, and snakelike lengths of cable swung from broken rafters. Lyn could not help flashing back to another hot, dark place filled with terror and the threat of imminent death, and yet...this time it was different. This time she wasn't alone.

They were almost side by side; Lyn's shoulders against Casey's hips as they inched through the opening toward the direction the dog had gone. She could hear the hiss of his breathing and feel the contraction of the muscles of his legs as he pulled himself along.

"And you're a crazy person," he replied tightly. "You've got no business in here, and there's a penalty for crossing a police barrier, much less—"

"You told me you didn't get involved," Lyn accused breathlessly, struggling to pull herself alongside him. "You didn't care. Everything's expendable to you, right, Mr. Carmichael? Because you don't get attached. But who is it who's risking his life to go after a dog that probably didn't survive the cave-in?"

Casey paused, and she felt him stiffen beside her. "He's not dead," he said, very lowly. "That stupid mutt of yours is on the trail of something, God knows how. And anyway..."

Lyn pulled herself up beside him, shoulder to shoulder, neck to neck. "You lied," she said. "You do care, and you care a lot about everything. It's all just an act, it has been from the beginning and you almost had me believing it, damn you."

When he turned his head his face was so close that his nose brushed hers and his lips were almost on hers. His breath flooded across her skin and his eyes were like embers, locking them together. She could feel the same adrenaline surging through him that was pumped in her veins, anger and passion, need and fear, desperate welcome and the fury of anxiety. He breathed, "If we ever get out of this, we're going to have a hell of a fight."

She replied grimly, "You'd better believe it."

And suddenly he tensed. "Quiet! I hear something."

She heard it, too, a frantic scratching and clawing punctuated by soft whining. They started to move forward again, more quickly now, and the fear that was pounding in Lyn's heart was sharp and urgent. The movements of a dog had set off the most recent collapse; the rubble was so fragilely balanced that even Rabbit, in his eagerness to find his self-proclaimed target, could precipitate another, perhaps even more serious accident.

They hoisted themselves over a broken culvert and they both saw Rabbit at once, pawing at a pile of broken boards and cement chunks. "Good dog!" Lyn gasped.

Casey extended his hand to the dog. "Here boy, that's enough—"

There was a shuddering, a creaking, a thundering explosion of dust and crackling debris. Lyn cried out and Casey swung around, pulling her into his arms and pushing them both against the far side of the culvert. He shielded her with his body and she tried to do the same for him as the loosely piled metal and plaster above them began to shift and give way, showering them with dust and gravel . . . and then was still.

They clung to each other with arms like steel; Casey could feel the thundering of her heartbeat and the slamming of his own. But she was alive. She was alive, safe, clinging to him; he couldn't distinguish her gasps for breath from his own and all he wanted to do was hold her, just hold her and never let her go. He couldn't pretend anymore. He couldn't hide anymore. He had never needed anything so intensely as he needed her in that moment, had never loved anyone so desperately . . .

"Lyn," he whispered. All the pain and loneliness of the past two weeks—of all his life—surged up within him then and he couldn't hold it back no matter how hard he tried. He closed his eyes tightly against an emotion almost too intense for him to bear, he ran his hands over her shoulders, her back, tangling them in her hair...just feeling her, holding her, keeping her close. Keeping her safe. "Oh, God, Lyn..."

"Say it," she whispered hoarsely. Her hands were moving across his back, his neck, his arms and his face with the same sort of fierce, wondrous urgency that was in his touch...just reassuring herself he was there and unharmed, that they were safe together. "Say it," she repeated. "I need to hear—"

"I love you!" His voice was a breathless half whisper at first, then stronger as his fingers tightened on her shoulders and pushed her a few inches away, his eyes blazing into hers. "I love you," he repeated distinctly, "and I'm not going to let you go, not now, not ever. Do you understand that?"

"I understand," she whispered, and they sank into each other's arms again, holding each other for one last moment of joy and discovery that was all too brief, but seemed to last forever.

And then, on a mutual instinct they moved apart, following the sounds of scuffling movement. When they traced the sound to its source it was just in time to see Rabbit scrambling past them toward the safety of the light outside. A grimness came into Casey's expression as he watched the dog go. "That," he said, breathing hard, "is not a good sign."

Their eyes met briefly, in undisguised fear and urgency, and without another word they moved forward and began to loosen the boards Rabbit had been clawing at.

At last they had created an opening large enough for Casey to wedge himself partway through. Lyn waited, straining and anxious, until she heard—she thought she heard—a muffled sound, like a whine.

"He's here!" Casey called. "He's alive."

Lyn released a quavering breath of relief. "Hurry," she said.

His head and shoulders were inside the opening, his arms stretched overhead. "Lyn—take off my shirt. Hand it to me. I can't—I don't want to let go of him."

Not hesitating to question, Lyn wedged her hands underneath him, tearing at the buttons of his shirt, pulling it off his body one sleeve at a time as he lowered his arms to her. She bundled up the material and passed it to him, then moved back, waiting once again.

"Do you know something?" Casey's voice was muffled and strained as it came to her. "We make a pretty good team."

Lyn massaged her aching throat. "That's what I've been trying to tell you," she whispered.

It seemed forever, though it actually couldn't have been more than a few minutes, before Casey appeared with Montana, muzzled by his shirt, in his arms. His face was taut and streaked with sweat, but his eyes were quietly triumphant. "Come on," he said, "let's get out of here."

Lyn went with them to the emergency clinic, where Montana was diagnosed as suffering from a simple femural break. Casey stayed with the dog as its leg was set, and Lyn stayed with Casey, holding his hand. The vet assured them that Montana would recover smoothly and regain full use of his leg in short order, but Lyn could see that Casey did not want to leave the dog, even overnight. He didn't say anything, and he put on his usual matter-of-fact front, but Lyn could tell.

The night was dark and starlit as they pulled up in front of Casey's house, Rabbit sitting on the front seat between them. Casey turned off the ignition and leaned his head back against the headrest, silent for a moment.

"I should take you back to your car," he said. "I don't know what I'm thinking about. You were crazy to come out there today."

"And you were crazy to think I wouldn't." Lyn opened the door and got out. Rabbit, apparently happy to be back in his second home, bounded out after her and made himself comfortable on a lounge chair on the porch.

Casey watched the dog with a smile as he got out of the car. "He doesn't look much like a hero now, does he?"

"All in a day's work," agreed Lyn. They went up the steps together and she paused to scratch Rabbit's ears. The dog looked at her, then closed his eyes again. "You were wrong about him, you know."

Casey unlocked the door. "Oh, yeah?"

"You said he couldn't be trained. That he was worthless. He wasn't worthless today."

"Well, I'll admit that, but his behavior wasn't all that extraordinary, you know. He heard the sound of another canine in distress and went to investigate. Any dog would do the same."

They stepped inside, and Casey switched on the light. Lyn turned to face him. "You were wrong about something else," she said. "You were wrong about me."

He had pulled on a light windbreaker over his bare chest, zipped halfway up. His hair was windblown and there was the slight bristle of a sandy beard on his lower jaw. He looked worn and rumpled and vulnerable, and Lyn had never loved anyone in all her life as much as she did him at that moment.

His face softened, and he reached out a hand for her. "Lyn, honey, I know..."

"No." She stiffened her shoulders and lifted her chin. "You promised me a fight, and I've got some things to say."

For a moment he stared at her, and then he spread his hands, managing a resigned smile. "Okay. Fight."

"You know what your trouble is, don't you?" she accused. "You've started to believe your own publicity. All this stuff about being perfect, being right, about never making a mistake—that's just for the dogs! You make them believe it because that's what you do, but let me tell you something, Casey, you are *not* perfect, and you *do* make mistakes!"

He frowned a little. "Lyn, I don't want to get into this..."

"You can't go around managing and manipulating people's lives, Casey! So maybe you were only doing what you thought was best, and maybe it *was* best—but not for me! Do you understand that?" She struck her chest. "Only *I* know what's best for *me*."

"Don't you see? That's what I was trying to—"

"And you know what else? The only reason you stay in control all the time is because you're afraid not to be! You were afraid to feel, to care, to get involved because you were afraid of losing. But you were only fooling yourself, Casey, and pushing aside all the good things you could have had because you're afraid to let go and open up."

"For God's sake, Lyn, don't you think I know that?" His face was pained now, his eyes stormy. "Don't you think these past two weeks—"

"And that's another thing!" She advanced a step on him. "I'd like to thank you for the most miserable two weeks of my life. While you were trying to do what was best for me you almost pushed me into making the worst decision I could have possibly made."

"I'm not responsible for—"

"You *are* responsible for me!" she cried. "Just like I'm responsible for you. Don't you know that by now? And we have to do what's best for *us*—for each other. I don't have to go to Philadelphia, I don't want to go to Philadelphia. That part of my life is over. I like working with animals, I like making a small difference in a small way. Maybe I'm not very good at it yet, but I can learn and, oh, Casey, don't you see? I don't want to change the world anymore, all I want to do is light a single candle. And I can do that here, with you."

She heard his sharp intake of breath, and saw the flicker of hope and question in his eyes. Once again he lifted his hand as though to reach for her, then let it drop. "Lyn, I—"

"And I'll tell you something else you were wrong about." She took another step toward him, fists clenched. "You said you didn't need me—"

"I never said that—"

"Perfect people don't need anyone, do they? That's the whole trouble!"

"I never said—"

"But you *do* need me! You needed me today, and you—"

He grabbed her arms and pulled her to him, closing her mouth with a kiss.

Passion flared hard and fast, searing her skin, exploding inside her head. "I do need you," he whispered against her mouth. Urgently his hand moved over her back and caught in her hair. "I need you so much I can't think straight..."

Lyn thrust her hands inside his open jacket, closing her fingers on hot, bare skin and tufted hair. Her voice was but a gasp as she sought his mouth again. "Why didn't you call me?"

"I almost did." His mouth closed on her neck, her throat, the lobe of her ear.

"I was home." Impatiently she tugged open the zipper of his jacket, bringing the full length of his exposed chest against her. Heat raged through her senses.

"I didn't know that." He pulled open the buttons of her shirt and his hands closed around her breasts. Dizziness soared. "I was afraid . . ."

She unsnapped his jeans, tugged at the zipper. "I couldn't leave. I told you I couldn't . . ."

"Lyn . . ." He groaned as his mouth covered hers once again and they fell to the sofa.

Her arms and legs wound around him and he was inside her in a swift hot explosion of blinding need, a storm of desperate demand that raged and crashed around them and swept them along, helpless against its power. Hands sought and grasped, muscles strained, hungry mouths drank of each other. The tide of sensation swept through them and shattered within them, leaving them lost amidst the whirling, scattered pieces of themselves, clinging only to each other.

They lay together amidst the tangle of their clothing, heartbeats thundering, breaths shallow and gasping, while the world slowly righted itself. Casey's fingers threaded through Lyn's, with his other hand he stroked her hair.

"Lyn," he whispered, "I'm sorry." His voice sounded dazed and stunned, as overwhelmed by what they had just shared as she was. "I didn't mean for it to be like that. I just . . . I guess I lost control."

Lyn smiled, and tightened her fingers on his. "I guess you did," she murmured. "And it's about time."

He released a breath, and rested his head beside hers, drawing her even closer against him. "I'm so glad you came back to me," he said.

Lyn propped herself up on her elbow, looking down at him, tracing the shape of his eyebrows with her finger. How she loved that face. She could spend the rest of her life looking at that face. "You were right about something, though," she said softly. "I do need to work with people, to help them . . . that's what I'm good at, what I know. But I'm good at other things, too, Casey. I want you to teach me how to train assistance dogs, and I want to work with the handicapped. That's the kind of difference I want to make."

He lifted his hand to caress her hair, smiling. "That's quite an undertaking. It'll take years of training before you're even qualified to place a dog."

"I know that."

"We'd have to spend a lot of time together."

"I think I could handle that."

His eyes were sober. "Are you sure? Because I meant what I said before, Lyn. I'm never letting go. I want you to marry me."

Her eyes closed against the joy that swelled inside her, but there was no holding back the smile. "Yes," she whispered, and her voice sounded a little choked. "I think I could handle that, too."

He drew her down on top of him, wrapping his arms around her, holding her securely against his chest. "I'm glad,'' he said softly. ''Because I don't think I can live without you.''

Lyn smiled, and snuggled contentedly against his shoulder. ''I know,'' she answered.

*   *   *   *   *

Available now from

SILHOUETTE® Desire™

MAN OF THE MONTH 1991

What's a hero? He's a man who's . . .

Handsome	Charming
Intelligent	Dangerous
Rugged	Enigmatic
Lovable	Adventurous
Tempting	Hot-blooded
Undoubtedly sexy	Irresistible

He's everything you want—and he's back! Twelve brand-new MAN OF THE MONTH heroes from twelve of your favorite authors . . .

NELSON'S BRAND by Diana Palmer	in January
OUTLAW by Elizabeth Lowell	in February
MCALLISTER'S LADY by Naomi Horton	in March
THE DRIFTER by Joyce Thies	in April
SWEET ON JESSIE by Jackie Merritt	in May
THE GOODBYE CHILD by Ann Major	in June

And that's just the beginning! So no matter what time of year, no matter what season, there's a dynamite MAN OF THE MONTH waiting for you . . . *only* in Silhouette Desire.

MOM91AR

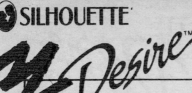

IT'S A CELEBRATION OF MOTHERHOOD!

Following the success of BIRDS, BEES and BABIES, we are proud to announce our second collection of Mother's Day stories.

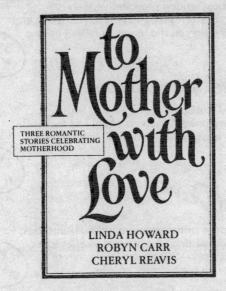

THREE ROMANTIC STORIES CELEBRATING MOTHERHOOD

to Mother with Love

LINDA HOWARD
ROBYN CARR
CHERYL REAVIS

Three stories in one volume, all by award-winning authors—stories especially selected to reflect the love all families share.

Available in May, TO MOTHER WITH LOVE is a perfect gift for yourself or a loved one to celebrate the joy of motherhood.

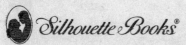

ML-1

FOUR UNIQUE SERIES
FOR EVERY WOMAN YOU ARE...

Silhouette Romance®

Love, at its most tender, provocative, emotional...in stories that will make you laugh and cry while bringing you the magic of falling in love.

6 titles per month

Silhouette Special Edition®

Sophisticated, substantial and packed with emotion, these powerful novels of life and love will capture your imagination and steal your heart.

6 titles per month

SILHOUETTE *Desire*®

Open the door to romance and passion. Humorous, emotional, compelling—yet always a believable and sensuous story—Silhouette Desire never fails to deliver on the promise of love.

6 titles per month

SILHOUETTE·INTIMATE·MOMENTS®

Enter a world of excitement, of romance heightened by suspense, adventure and the passions every woman dreams of. Let us sweep you away.

4 titles per month

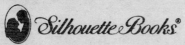